Nevada Heat

Book Three
David Huff

Copyright © 2017

Published by David Huff - Publishing — Ephraim, UT
 ISBN: 978-0-9988003-2-5
Library of Congress Control Number: 2018901530
Nevada Heat/ David Huff
Digital distribution | David Huff, 2017.
Paperback Edition | David Huff, 2017

This is a work of fiction. The characters, names, incidents, places, and dialogue are products of the author's imagination, and are not to be construed as real.

Previous Books in the Heat Series
Arizona Heat
Florida Heat
Nevada Heat

Chinese Proverb:

Man has the limitless capacity to achieve
goodness.

This book is dedicated to the law-enforcement organizations throughout the United States who put their lives on the line every day 24/7 to protect us from the bad guys so that we can have a good life to live and our dreams fulfilled.

Chapter I

As Miguel was walking up Fremont Street in Las Vegas, Nevada, in and out of the crowds that were either coming or going to one of the casinos along the route, he noticed he was being followed by two men dressed in typical evening attire. They were wearing windbreakers, slacks and sunglasses. The sunglasses were what caught Miguel's eye as he walked by the Golden Nugget Hotel and Casino towards the Union Plaza Hotel, which was located at the top of Fremont Street and was the beginning of the famous Las Vegas Strip.

Miguel had enrolled at the University of Nevada Las Vegas (UNLV) for a master's in business management program the year before and was almost done with his first year. The lights of the big city of Las Vegas are what attracted him to go to UNLV. Buck and Rachael tried to talk him out of going to UNLV when he could stay home and continue at Arizona State University (ASU) for the same degree for a lot less money. Being adamant, going with his friends to UNLV proved to be the greater enticement. However, that was a year ago, but tonight he was concentrating on trying to get away from the two men following him.

Miguel went into one of the casinos to see if he could shake the two men and got caught up in a crowd of people watching one of the gamblers, supposedly winning money at one of the quarter slot machines. With the bells ringing and the red lights flashing, the crowd gathered around watching just to see how much money the person had won, hoping they could catch the money that fell on the floor. The two men were there as well, watching Miguel and not the least bit interested in the crowd of onlookers. He realized he wouldn't be able to lose these two without doing something drastic to get away. He knew he couldn't outrun them and he wasn't sure if they were carrying guns. Miguel reached into where the money was falling into the bottom of the slot machine, grabbed a handful of quarters and threw them into the air. This set off a frenzy for the spectators as they started reaching for the money in the air and on the ground. With all the confusion going on, Miguel slipped out of the crowd and went into the back of the casino, leaving the two men fighting to get through the ever-increasing crowd of greedy gamblers. After finding another exit, Miguel slipped out through the back door of the casino. He waited in the shadows behind some of the dumpsters, to see if the two men were still following him. After waiting a couple of minutes to be certain he wasn't being followed anymore, he made his way to his car and drove back to the university. When he got to his apartment, he went in and locked the door behind him before turning out the light and going to sleep.

Chapter II

The next morning, Miguel woke up to someone knocking on his door. Quickly getting dressed, he shuffled to the door, opened it and found Marissa standing there. Miguel looked at her for a second and realized that he had forgotten about picking her up for school so they could go to class together. He looked sheepishly at her and started to apologize, but it was too late for that now. She walked in, her blue eyes were lit up for war. Her blond hair was windblown from the walk over to his apartment. She sat down on the couch, not saying a word while she glared at Miguel. Miguel looked at her and stammered the words, "I'm sorry."

Marissa was not going to accept only one "I'm sorry" today, and Miguel, looking at her, understood that. Marissa was pretty upset and Miguel could see that it was hopeless to try and explain anything to her at this point. So Miguel left the room and went in and changed his clothes to get ready for class.

When he came out, Marissa was still on the

couch, and her being mad had cooled down to a slightly agitated state. Marissa looked at Miguel and asked, "What happened that you forgot to pick me up this morning?"

Miguel stammered a little, "I ran into a little trouble last night; I had two men following me and …."

"Why would two men be following you?" She blurted out.

"I don't know."

"Are you telling me the truth, or is this your way of getting out of trouble with me?"

"I swear, it's the truth."

Now Marissa looked concerned, and all of the mad was gone, being replaced with, "Are you all right?" and "What happened?"

Miguel explained the whole incident to her from the beginning. By now Marissa was moving closer to kiss him. Miguel was on Marissa's good side now. After a couple of minutes of talking they both went down to his car and drove to their class at UNLV.

After class was over Miguel and Marissa walked to the commons area to eat lunch, their daily ritual had started. Finding a table, they sat down with their lunch and proceeded to eat. As they were eating, Marissa asked Miguel, "Did you forget, you're meeting my parents tonight?"

"I've not forgotten; it's at your place tonight, and you're fixing dinner for all of us."

"I know my parents are going to like you. All you got to do is sit there and be cute."

With that, Miguel started to blush a little and smiled. Marissa continued, "My dad is the one you have to impress the most. You're dating his little girl and he wants to make sure you're good enough to be dating me."

All Miguel could do at this point was listen to Marissa. When Marissa smiled that special smile at Miguel, his heart would melt. For him it was love at first sight. She was the light of his life. They had met at a dance which was held on campus, and from that point on they had become inseparable. They discovered that they were both going for their master's degrees, but in different programs. She wanted to be a social worker, working with kids in difficult family situations, and Miguel was going for his Master of Business Administration (MBA), planning to use it in law enforcement. Some of the classes were common core for both their degrees, and that's why they were together in this one class. Miguel knew he was going to marry her, which he had decided would have to wait until he finished his master's degree. The hard part for him would be to introduce Marissa to his parents, Buck, and Rachael, and get their approval.

Buck and Rachael had become the parents that Miguel never had. They taught him about America and gave him all the love he needed to live in a strange land. Miguel had exceeded his learning by passing his GED quickly and then enrolling at ASU as a foreign student. Miguel was able to use his Spanish language to his advantage in the College Level Examination Program to satisfy his language requirements and to get started in his criminal justice program. With a lot of hard work and with Buck and Rachael's assistance with the classes, he quickly mastered the courses and was able to graduate and get accepted to an MBA program at UNLV. It took four years for him to get his criminal justice degree, but with the support he had from Buck and Rachael the years went by quickly. Now here he is with the love of his life, getting ready to meet his sweetheart's parents for the first time. Miguel felt nervous already, thinking about tonight. That's when Marissa reached out and touched his hand, telling him it was going to be all right. His heart melted again and he felt that maybe this would work out tonight.

As they finished their lunch, Miguel and

Marissa were done for the day, as far as classes went. They gathered up their school work and headed to the car. The rest of the day Miguel would be helping Marissa get everything that she needed to cook for dinner tonight to impress her parents. He enjoyed being with her, even when it came to shopping. In the part of Colombia he was from they didn't have the grocery stores like they had here in Las Vegas. To him, it was still an adventure to walk around inside, seeing the different fruits and vegetables from places he never knew existed. Walking up and down the aisles, Miguel was amazed at all the different packaged food located in one place. He had discovered that his favorite food in America was peanut butter-and-jam sandwiches. Marissa took him by the hand as they walked into the store. Miguel grabbed a cart and was happy following her up and down the aisles as she checked off her list the things she needed to buy for tonight's dinner.

When they were done shopping, they went to her apartment. Miguel got roped into helping Marissa fix dinner by cutting the potatoes into quarters for the cooking pot. As far as Miguel was concerned, he was living the dream with Marissa and he loved it all. While cutting the potatoes, Miguel's cell phone started to ring. He looked at his phone and saw that it was his friend Tim calling.

"Hello, Tim; what's up?"

"I need to talk to you about something very important right away. When can we get together to meet?"

Miguel looked at Marissa, who was busy chopping onions for tonight's salad. "How about tomorrow after class?"

"That will be too late for me. How about I meet you at the library on campus later tonight?"

Miguel begged off. "I'm helping Marissa get dinner ready for her parents tonight; it will have to wait till tomorrow after class."

"All right then. Meet me tomorrow in the library after class."

After dinner was prepared and put on the stove to cook, Miguel assisted Marissa with setting the table. Now It was Marissa who was getting nervous about her parents meeting Miguel. Miguel, taking her hand, and sitting with her on the couch, tried to calm her down.

Later that evening Marissa's parents showed up for dinner. She introduced Miguel to both her mom and dad, and as they sat down at the table, her dad asked Miguel, "Do you like to go fishing?"

"Mom, can't you stop him; he's embarrassing me again," Marissa said as she looked at her mom.

Miguel wasn't sure what to make of her dad's question and answered, "Yes, I do like to fish."

"Not now, dear," Marissa's mom said.

Her dad smiled, but kept quiet after that.

"So how is it you came to America, Miguel?" Marissa's mom asked.

Miguel looked at Marissa's mom and thought for a moment, then proceeded to tell his story about what happened to him and his parents and how he met and saved Buck and Rachael from the cartel while they were in Colombia, working for the FBI. After hearing his story, her parents looked at Marissa as her mom said, "You're lucky to have this young man in your life."

Marissa and Miguel both smiled at her comment.

"I know I am, and that's why I love him," Marissa said.

After dinner was over and her parents had gone, Miguel asked Marissa while they were cleaning up, "Why did your dad ask me about fishing?"

"Every time I brought home a date the first thing he would do is ask if they liked to go fishing. My boyfriends would sometimes say "yes" and sometimes they would say "no." Then he would ask them if they had ever been shark fishing? And, of course, the boys would say "no." Then my father would ask them how long they could tread water? The boys would look at him kind of strange. Then my dad would say, "If you don't bring my daughter home on time we may need to go shark fishing." Then he would ask again how long they could tread water. It was his way of making sure I got home on time from my dates. As you can probably tell, I didn't have too many dates with the same guys after that."

Miguel thought about it for a minute and laughed when he heard this. "I think I like your father."

Later that night, after leaving Marissa's place, Miguel went back to his own apartment. As he was about to lay down and go to sleep, there was a knock on the door. Opening the door, he saw Tim with his girlfriend, Jennifer, holding him up against the door frame. Miguel looked at Tim and saw that he had a fat lip, a swollen eye, and a busted nose. Jennifer pushed past Miguel and took Tim to the couch to lay him down. Miguel looked at Tim, surprised by all the damage done to his face. "What happened to him?"

"I don't know; all I do know is he came to my place looking like this and he told me to bring him here," Jennifer said, looking up at Miguel.

Miguel moved a little closer to look at Tim. He could see that he was fading in and out and was incoherent in his speaking. Jennifer was pretty upset seeing him like this. Miguel could tell she didn't know what to do. He put his arm around her. "He'll be fine, he just needs a little time to heal up. You were right to bring him here."

Miguel started thinking about the other night on Fremont Street and being followed by the two men wearing sunglasses. He wondered if this had anything to do with what had just happened to Tim.

"Who would do something like this to Tim?" Miguel asked.

"I don't know."

"Jennifer, has anything unusual happened to either of you lately?"

She shook her head no. "Nothing I can think of, except maybe when we went on our day trip to Death Valley and saw Scotty's Castle."

"What was unusual about that?"

"We were late getting away from Death Valley, and as we were driving home after sunset, we saw this Cessna flying around real low to the ground. We decided to follow it with our car and see where it went. After following it for a while the plane landed. The funny thing was, there appeared to be a landing strip of some sort out there in the middle of the desert because we could see flares running parallel out there on the desert floor. As the plane came to a stop, we got out of our car to see if it was in trouble. We walked over to where we the thought the plane was, and as we got closer we saw a van and some men unloading something out of the plane and putting it into the van. Tim decided he wanted to get pictures of what was going on with his cell phone. As he was taking a picture, the flash from the cell phone got one of the men's attention and they started chasing after us. When we got to our car, we took off as fast as we could."

Miguel knew exactly what had happened, "Do you think anybody recognized you while you were driving away?"

"I don't know; all I know is that Tim said he felt like somebody had been following him for the last couple of days."

"You guys watched a drug plane unload its cargo, and now they're after you for the pictures you took of them. Does Tim have the cell phone he used to take the pictures?"

"He used my cell phone; his phone didn't have enough of a battery charge left on it."

Miguel wasn't sure what to do at this point in time. He was concerned if the two men knew where he lived, and if so, he needed to find out if they knew where Marissa lived, as well. There wasn't anything that could be done for Tim right now, except to let him heal and rest. He wondered if they needed to find another place to hide. He decided to call Buck and ask him what to do. Using his cell phone, he waited for Buck or Rachael to answer the phone. To Miguel, it seemed quite a long time before Rachael finally answered.

"Hello, son, how are you?" Rachael asked.

"Well, I'm kind of in a jam right now and I need your help to figure out what to do. One of my friends got caught taking photos of a drug drop in the desert a couple of days ago. He got beat up pretty bad after they found him. I'm not sure what to do at this point. Also, there were a couple of guys following me the other night on Fremont Street. I was able to shake them, but I'm concerned that they might know where I live and come after me, as well."

"Wait a minute; I'll get your dad on the phone, too."

A minute later, Buck and Rachael were both on the phone, talking to Miguel about the situation he now found himself in with his friends. "Do you think you can come down here to stay while we sort this out?" Buck asked.

"I don't know for sure. I think they might try to follow us. Can you guys come up and get us?"

"That's a possibility. That way we'll be sure you and your friends will be safe," Rachael said.

After discussing their options, it was decided that the best course of action was for Buck and Rachael to go up to Vegas and get the kids. "In the meantime, I will call one of my friends up there to come over and keep an eye on you until we get there," Buck said.

"Thanks, mom and dad, for being there."

"That's what parents do for their kids," Rachael said.

After the phone call, Miguel checked on Tim again, asking Jennifer, "How's he doing?"

Jennifer looked at Miguel with tears in her eyes. "No change so far; I think he may be getting worse."

As Miguel walked around his apartment, he started turning the lights off. Looking through the blinds, he checked the parking lot below, looking for something, anything out of place.

He pulled the curtains closed, and out of the corner of the blinds he kept watch. There was nothing for them to do, except wait for Buck and Rachael to come. As the hours went on, he and Jennifer took turns watching out the window. His cell phone rang, and recognizing the ring tone, he flipped it open to answer, "Hello, Dad."

"Is everything still okay? I've got some bad news: My friend is on vacation and isn't in the area. I've called the police department, and after explaining to them your situation, the best that they could offer was a metro unit doing a drive-by."

"I haven't seen any police cars come by at all."

"Have you seen anything unusual since we talked last?"

"Nothing out of the ordinary. Wait a minute; Jennifer is motioning for me to come over to look out the window. Hang on," he walked over and peered out the side of the window.

A second later he was back on the phone with Buck and Rachael, "There's a car that just pulled into the parking lot with two men in it, just sitting and watching. I think it's the same two men that I saw the other night."

"Can you and your friends get out of the apartment without being seen?"

Miguel thought a minute. "I think we can."

By now Buck was getting a little excited. "Can you see the license plate on the car? If so, copy it down and see if you can get out of there with your friends. Call me when you're safe."

"Okay, we're on our way out now."

"Be careful, son; we'll be there as soon as we can."

Miguel picked up Tim, as Jennifer got on the other side of Tim to help him move. With the lights out, the entranceway to Miguel's apartment was completely dark.

"Jennifer, where did you park your car?" Miguel asked.

"Down in front, next to the car with the two men in it."

Miguel frowned and Jennifer started to cry. Miguel looked at Jennifer. "Now is not the time to start crying. I need you to help me get Tim out of the apartment to a safe place."

With that, Jennifer quit crying. "Okay."

Miguel knew his car was out front, as well, and getting to either car would be impossible without being seen. Miguel slowly opened the door to his apartment. Once outside, they carefully moved Tim down the hallway, making sure that they made no noise that would attract the attention of the two men in the car. When they were down on the street level, they went through the back area, past the fence, and made their way to a local convenience store across the street. They stopped there while Miguel called Marissa on the phone.

Marissa, waking up to her phone ringing next to her bed and still being half asleep, said, "Hello, who is this?"

Miguel identified himself over the phone. "This is Miguel and I need your help right now."

"Miguel, do you know what time it is? It's the middle of the night!"

"Marissa, this is important. Listen, you need to come down to the convenience store behind my apartment complex. It's a matter of life and death."

Marissa, fully awake now, "Miguel if you're joking, I'm going to get you for this."

"You need to hurry, please. This is no joke. And stay away from my apartment."

"Oh, all right, I'll be right down, but you better not be joking."

In about ten minutes, Marissa pulled into the convenience store and got out of the car to look for Miguel. Miguel called to Marissa from the shadows next to the building, and as she walked to where he was, she could see Jennifer and Miguel holding Tim.

"What's going on?" she asked excitedly when

she saw everybody hiding there in the dark.

Miguel looked around to make sure Marissa wasn't followed by anyone. Making sure, he asked Marissa to get back in the car and wait a minute. Marissa did as she was told and was waiting in the car when Miguel and Jennifer brought Tim to the car and put him in the back seat. Jennifer crawled in next to Tim, and Miguel got in the passenger seat in front. At this point Marissa looked at Tim, "What happened to Tim?"

"I'll explain everything to you as you drive. Now you need to get going for everybody's sake," Miguel said.

As she drove the car, Miguel explained what had happened to Tim and why it happened.

"Where do you want me to drive to?" Marissa asked Miguel.

"I don't rightly know at this time; just keep driving."

Miguel pulled out his cell phone and called Buck and Rachael. "Just to let you know that we're okay and were out of the apartment."

"That's good, son. We're about two hours away from Vegas and I need you to find a safe place to hole up in until we get there," Buck said.

"I'm not sure if they know where Marissa

lives. If we go to her apartment, chances are they could be waiting for us there, too."

"Agreed. How about a friend or somebody that you can trust, that you haven't seen in a while?"

Miguel thought about it and asked Marissa, "Do you have any friends that you know and trust, that we could go and visit tonight, on short notice?"

"I know this one family really well that would let us stay for a couple of hours, if need be."

Miguel got back on the phone. "We found a place and we can meet you there."

"Good, when we get to town, I'll call you again to get the address, all right?" Buck replied.

"Okay, we'll be waiting for your call."

Marissa turned the car around and headed into West Las Vegas, down Lake Mead Blvd., and within minutes they pulled in front of a house that looked like a mansion. It was surrounded by cinder-block walls on three sides with palm trees in front of the house.

"I hope they're home. Stay here until I come back to get you guys," Marissa said to Miguel.

With that, Marissa was out of the car and up to the door of the house in ten seconds flat. Miguel watched her as she rang the doorbell. The curtain next to door opened and you could see the man of the house was in his pajamas and robe, looking out the side window to see who it was. Upon recognizing Marissa, he opened the door and let her in. A few minutes later the door opened again, and the wife of the man was with him. Marissa came running back to the car. "It's all right. You can come in now."

Miguel helped Jennifer get Tim out of the car and slowly move him up to the house. When the couple saw the shape Tim was in, they came out to help bring him inside.

After getting Tim upstairs and into bed, the mom shooed everybody out of the room, except for Jennifer. With a last look inside, the mom closed the door behind her and went downstairs to meet everybody there. Marissa introduced Gared and Tina to the kids standing in the room, "These two people here are like my extra mom and dad when my parents are not around."

Gared and Tina had been friends of Marissa's parents for years and had watched Marissa as a child grow up before their eyes. With that, Miguel introduced himself as Marissa's boyfriend and then introduced Jennifer, pointing upstairs, as Tim's girlfriend from school.

"What happened to Tim?" Gared asked.

Miguel and Marissa explained as best as they could about the beating Tim had received, the drug plane, and how they ended up here at their home.

Tina went into the kitchen and fixed some food for the kids and brought it out for them to eat.

"One of my friends is a doctor; I don't think he would mind coming over to look at Tim tonight." Gared said.

"That would be great; I'm really worried about him," Miguel said.

Gared was gone in a flash and back with the cell phone, calling his friend. "Bob, this is Gared. I need you to come over as soon as you can. We have a boy over here that's been pretty badly beaten up." After a pause Gared said, "That would be fine," and closed his phone. Gared looked at Miguel, who had been listening to the conversation, "He'll be right over."

After a few minutes of small talk about school and life in general, the doorbell rang and Gared went to the door to answer it. Gared returned and introduced Bob to the kids.

"Where's the boy I need to see?" Bob asked Gared.

"I'll show you," Tina said, as she led the doctor upstairs with Marissa following behind her.

After a few minutes Tina and Marissa came

back down and waited with the rest of them while the doctor did his examination on Tim. In 15 minutes the doctor was coming down the stairs with Jennifer, saying, "Tim is a very lucky boy; most of the damage is superficial, except for his broken nose. He will heal and just have the memory of the beating. Fortunately for him, he is young and will recover quickly," looking at the others he continued, "Jennifer has all of my instructions as to what Tim will need for the next couple of days. I suggest you don't move him any more than what is needed, for his sake. I gave him a shot of Demerol and that should help with the pain for tonight. If you need anything else, let me know and I will come back as soon as I can. Goodnight."

Gared showed him to the door. "Thanks, Bob; we really appreciate this."

"It's my first time doing a house call; kind of nice, if I do say so myself."

Both men chuckled at Bob's remark. "I'll try not to make it a habit, Bob."

Gared shut the door behind him and came back into the front room. Tina looked at the kids and could see they were tired and ready to sleep. With the help of Marissa they found some sleeping bags and pillows for the kids so they could go to bed. Miguel was the only one who decided to stay up and wait for his dad's phone call. He asked Gared for their address and wrote it down, keeping it handy for his dad's phone call. Gared and Tina said goodnight to everybody and headed off to their own bedroom, turning out the lights as they went.

Marissa stayed next to Miguel as they sat on the couch. As she nodded off, she put her head on Miguel's shoulder and within seconds she was sound asleep. Miguel thought about everything that had transpired this evening, and remembering his own upbringing in Colombia, it brought back some bad experiences that somehow he had forgotten about since coming to America. He thought to himself, each place has its own bad stuff to deal with and, in some cases, it's not much different than what he had experienced in Colombia. As he sat there, he fell asleep waiting for the phone call. When his cell phone rang, he jumped and almost woke up Marissa. He answered the phone and it was Buck on the other end of the line. "Hello, where are you?"

"We're on I-15 going through the city; where are you?" Buck asked.

Miguel gave him the address to the house and Rachael plugged it into their GPS. After a minute the GPS showed the address and length of time it would take to get there. Rachael gave the driving instructions to Buck, after which he said, "We'll see you in a couple of minutes."

Chapter III

Hanging up the phone, Miguel felt better already. If anybody could help them in this situation, it would be Buck and Rachael. After what seemed an eternity, Miguel looked outside and saw the truck that belonged to Buck pull up in front of the house. Miguel opened the door, and before they even got halfway up the driveway, ran out and hugged them both, relieved to see them.

Rachael looked at Miguel, checking him over to make sure for herself that Miguel was okay; and having satisfied her motherly instinct, she let Buck talk to him.

"What happened after the phone call?" Buck asked.

Miguel explained how they were able to get away and how Marissa drove them to Gared and Tina's home, and about Tim who was upstairs in one of the rooms, recovering from the beating. Being fully updated, Buck and Rachael looked relieved and happy that all was good for now. They would look into it more closely later in the morning. In about three hours the sun would be coming up, and a new day would start in the valley. Buck and Rachael were able to find a place to sleep, and now that they were here, Miguel was able to sleep as well.

Later that morning, Gared came downstairs and saw that two new guests were there. Miguel introduced his parents to Gared, "Gared, these two new strangers in your house are my parents, Buck and Rachael."

Gared stuck out his hand and Buck took it to shake it. "I'm sorry for the circumstances, but I'm sure glad to meet you two," Gared said.

"Thank you, Gared, for allowing our son and his friends a place to stay for the night, and keeping them safe," Rachael replied.

By now Tina came down the stairs, "I checked on Tim; he seems to be doing better. Poor Jennifer hasn't left his side all night. She's still up there with him."

Gared introduced Tina to Buck and Rachael, and after the introductions Rachael asked, "Do you need any help in the kitchen for breakfast?"

"With this many people, I sure could," Tina said.

With that, the ladies went into the kitchen to prepare a meal for everybody there. Gared and Buck were able to finally speak in private about the situation.

"Gared, how bad is this?" Buck asked.

"I'm sure it's like what you have in Arizona, the gangs and such, peddling the drugs. Personally, I'm surprised that Tim is still alive after being seen by the men at the drop site," Gared replied.

"Me, too."

Rachael brought some coffee to Gared and Buck to start the day for them. Buck looked at Rachael. "I want you to know you look beautiful in the morning."

Rachael blushed. "I bet you say that to all of the ladies."

"Just the one I love," Buck smiled.

Gared smiled and sat there, drinking his coffee. After a few minutes Marissa was awake and was introduced to Buck and Rachael. Marissa felt embarrassed to be waking up in front of Miguel's parents, looking the way she did. Rachael looked at her, smiling, "So you're the one my son keeps going on about?"

Marissa turned red, feeling put on the spot, and smiled.

"Did Miguel ever tell you how we met him in Colombia?" Rachael asked as she put her arm around Marissa, taking her to the kitchen to help with breakfast. They became close friends from that point on.

As Jennifer was walking down the stairs, she said, "Tim is starting to come around a little bit and is able to talk now."

"I'll go up and see if I can talk to him and find out what happened," Buck said.

In about 30 minutes the table was set and everybody was there to sit down and eat. The typical breakfast for such a large crowd was hotcakes with eggs and orange juice. Everybody ate and Tina and Rachael refilled the hotcake plate three times to feed them all. When everybody was done, the girls started to clean up the mess in the kitchen, with help from Miguel doing the dishes.

Rachael looked at Marissa, "Miguel must like you a lot," looking at Miguel while he was helping Marissa do the dishes. She continued saying, "I could never get him the kitchen unless it was to try the food before we ate." Miguel blushed, Marissa smiled, and Rachael laughed.

Buck came down from Tim's room with a look of concern on his face. By now Rachael was out of the kitchen and coming into the front room. After seeing the look on Buck's face, she asked, "What's wrong?"

"The two men who did this got Tim's cell phone, thinking the pictures are on his phone, which they're not. The pictures are on Jennifer's phone and once they realize they've got the wrong phone, they'll be coming to find Jennifer and get her phone."

"That's not good for anybody. What do we do now?"

Buck called Jennifer over, "Can I see your phone for a minute?"

She pulled it from her pocket and gave it to Buck, who turned it on and started going through the pictures on her phone. When he found the pictures of the airplane and men unloading the drugs from the plane, he studied them for a couple of minutes.

"Is there a store around here where we can get these pictures printed?" Buck asked Gared.

"Yes, there is; down on Lake Mead Boulevard there is a shopping center. When you get to Lake Mead Blvd., turn right. You can't miss it."

Jennifer went with Buck to get into the truck and drive to find the shopping center. In a short time Buck and Jennifer returned to the house with the pictures from the phone. Showing the pictures to Rachael, she could see why the two men were after Tim and Jennifer. The pictures showed not only the van but the license plate on the van and the tail number of the plane. The faces of the men were slightly blurred but clear enough to identify them and what they were doing.

Buck looked at Rachael, "For being crazy for taking the pictures, Tim did a good job getting the right information to burn these guys. Too bad it almost cost him his life."

"We need to turn these pictures over to the police, or maybe the FBI," Rachael said.

"I agree. First thing this morning we'll go to the FBI."

"Just give me some time to get cleaned up before we go."

About 9:00 am Rachael and Buck were down at the office of the FBI, waiting to talk to the special agent in charge. When the agent was off the phone, the secretary, Sherron, said they could go in. Walking into the agent's office, the agent stood up, "I'm Special Agent Warren. How can I help you today?"

Buck introduced himself and Rachael to him. "I think you might be interested in these pictures we just had printed."

Handing the pictures to Warren, the agent started studying them, and after a minute he got on his phone and asked Sherron to please send in Jenkins.

"Where did you get these pictures?" Warren asked.

"A kid and his date took these pictures on the way back from Scotty's Castle about a week ago. The only problem was that they were seen, and the boy got himself beat up pretty bad for it," Rachael said.

"Who are you, again?" Warren asked.

"Our names are Buck and Rachael Tanner," Rachael answered.

Warren thought a moment about their names. "By chance, you guys aren't from Arizona, are you?"

Buck and Rachael both nodded their heads yes.

"There was a Buck Tanner and an FBI agent that busted up a county sheriff's drug operation down there. Are you the ones who did that?" Warren asked.

Again, Buck and Rachael nodded yes.

Warren stood up and shook their hands. "I've wanted to meet you two for a long time; you guys are legends around here."

With that, there was a knock on the door and Warren said, "Enter, Jenkins. I want you to meet two legends from Arizona, Buck and Rachael Tanner."

Jenkins looked at the two of them, and his eyes got big when he realized who they were. "We studied you guys at the academy when I was there a year ago."

Buck and Rachael smiled. And Buck, looking at Warren, interrupted Jenkins, "What about the pictures you have there?"

At this point, Warren cleared his throat and handed the pictures to Jenkins. "I want you to run the license plate and tail number of the plane down for me. Plus, see if you can get with the computer geeks and run a face-recognition program on the men in these pictures."

Jenkins looked at the pictures for a second and Warren looked at him. "Maybe sometime today, Jenkins."

Jenkins looked up and excused himself and left the room. Warren laughed, "Rookies, they're all the same. In fact, I think I was too, at one time or another."

Buck and Rachael left Warren's office with a promise that Warren would be in touch with them if anything came up. As they were leaving the building, Buck asked Rachael, "Do you ever miss being an agent?"

Rachael thought about it for a minute. "I would miss being married to you more," and kissed him.

When they got back to Gared and Tina's house, Tina came up to them with a message. "You need to call the FBI and here is their number. They sure sounded pretty excited about wanting to talk to you guys."

"Thank you. Do you have a place that is private where I could call them?" Buck asked.

"The den is the about the best private place we have. It's over in that direction."

Buck and Rachael went to find the den, and doing so, Buck dialed the number given to him and waited for Warren to pick up the phone. Warren's secretary answered the phone and patched him through to Warren's office. Warren was relieved to finally get hold of Buck and Rachael on the phone. He started off saying, "I'm glad you called back, I thought maybe you were on your way back to Arizona. Anyway, the face recognition came back on the pictures, as well as the license plate number. One face belongs to a man called Ice Man. He has been responsible for all of the drug trade in the Las Vegas area for the last five years. The car belongs to another dealer, who works the Strip with the prostitutes. He's nothing more than a pimp with a bad attitude. We've been trying to nail these guys for months, and you got them on film red-handed, loading the drugs into the van. How sweet it is to have it on film."

Rachael and Buck were pleased with the new information Warren had given them.

"So why are you calling us about this?" Buck asked.

"That was the good news; the bad news is that, because of the pictures, there is a bounty on not only Tim and Jennifer but Miguel, as well, to kill them because they could testify against them in court."

Rachael and Buck sat there, stunned by what Warren had just told them. "Why Miguel? He had nothing to do with this," said Buck.

"You know how they work; they're making a statement, and this is what they do best, using intimidation, violence and murder to accomplish it."

Rachael started to cry, and Buck started getting upset. Buck asked, "You've got the pictures as proof. Why can't you pick them up and jail them?"

"That wouldn't change anything. As long as those kids are out there and as long as the pictures exist, they are a threat to Ice Man and the pimp. Even if they are both in jail awaiting the court date, they can still call the shots. And not knowing how long it will be before going to court, no one would be safe."

What are you going to do about it?" cried Rachael.

"With the pictures, we have enough to go after

these guys and lock them up and throw away the keys. That being said, we are looking for them now and so is Metro Police Department. Nobody knows where they went or where they may be hiding. We know they're under a rock somewhere here in town, but that's all we know for certain."

"Any suggestions that may be of help?" Buck asked.

"Keep a close eye on the kids, and don't go anywhere unless you really need to. Oh, one other thought: We can put them in a safe house with a protection detail, if you like," Warren said.

"Would it do any good?" Buck asked.

"Not really. We've been having problems with our Intel being compromised in the past. I can't promise you they would be safer with us or with you. In my opinion, they're better off with you two than they would be with us."

Buck looked at Rachael and rolled his eyes from what Warren had said. "What do you suggest, then?"

"Well, for certain, they are safer with you two for now. We are drawing up the indictments from the U.S. Attorney General as we speak, and the court date is being set up as well. The only problem is we can't move forward without them being incarcerated first. I suggest you stay low until we catch them, and then we can expedite the case and they'll be in jail the whole time awaiting the trial."

"With their goons coming after the kids to kill them?" Rachael asked.

Warren didn't say a thing to what Rachael said, except, "We will do our best to get them; that's all I can promise you for now."

"Thank you for the heads up, Warren, and by the way, what's the name of the pimp?" Buck asked.

"He goes by the name of Mako. That's all we know about him for sure," Warren replied.

"Again, thanks for the heads up; we'll be in touch," Buck said as he hung up the phone.

Buck and Rachael were visibly shaken by the conversation, with Rachael being the worst for it. Buck took her and held her as she cried until she regained control. All Buck could say was, "It's going to be all right."

With that, Rachael exploded. "How do you know that! Are you some kind of mystic fortune teller that can see the future?"

Buck looked at her and said nothing. He too was upset and understood what Rachael was feeling and agreed with her. After she settled down and was ready to listen, Buck said, "We can keep them safe as long as we keep our cool. If we don't do that, they are as good as dead and, for that matter, so are we."

"Do you have an idea of what to do?"

"Not a clue; I'm making this up as we go."

"I thought you were really a fortune teller and had all of the ideas," Rachael said as she smiled.

"I wish I did this one time," Buck laughed.

"I wish you did, too. These poor kids don't realize what they've gotten themselves into, do they?"

"I think they're beginning to understand a little, with Tim getting beat up and people following them. Reality has a way of doing that."

"What can we do, Buck? I've never felt so helpless before."

"I have never liked being hunted by anyone. How about we become the hunters and take care of them ourselves?"

Rachael thought about this for a moment. "Better to do something than hide and do nothing, except wait for the police to catch them. When do we start hunting?"

"Once Tim is in shape to go to Arizona. In the meantime, we sit tight."

"Works for me," Rachael said, still being held by Buck.

After the phone call, Buck and Rachael talked to Tina about their phone call from the FBI agent and the situation they were in. Tina sat and listened for the better part of 30 minutes before saying anything.

"Are we safe here?" Tina asked them, sounding concerned.

"For the time being we are. Rachael and I will be going out this evening to see if we can find out anything. Until then we need to get some sleep," Buck replied.

"Mi casa es su casa; please make yourselves at home," Tina said.

With that, she showed them another room where they could sleep. Buck and Rachael lay down and tried to sleep, knowing it would be a while for that to happen. Before to long they had drifted off to sleep.

At 9:00 pm Buck and Rachael decided it was time to go out for the night and look for Mako. All they knew for sure was he worked the Strip with his girls and the best way to find him was to find one of his working girls. Before they left, they checked with Tina to see how Tim was doing.

"He seems to be improving every day; pretty soon he will be ready to go home," Tina said.

Buck looked at her, "Where is Gared? I need

to talk to him."

"He's in the family room right now watching TV," replied Tina.

Buck and Rachael walked into the family room, where Gared was sitting. "We have a situation here you need to be aware of, Gared."

Gared looked up, "What about?"

"We don't know if Tina mentioned this to you, but earlier today we received a phone call from the FBI. We need you to be aware of what's going on." At this point, Buck and Rachael explained what they had learned from the phone call they had received from the FBI and the ramifications of it.

At the end of the conversation Gared asked, "Tina told me about this, what do you need me to do?"

"Try to keep the kids here as best as you can. Don't let them go out alone, unless it's with one of you two. At this point, we don't know what or who they've been seen by, so to be safe, keep them here, at least until we know more," Rachael said.

Gared looked at them, and sensing their concern for the kids, said, "Not a problem; we can do that."

"Have you seen Miguel lately?" Buck asked Gared.

"He's in the kitchen with Marissa right now, eating."

Rachael and Buck went to the kitchen and found Miguel and Marissa eating some leftovers. Rachael came and gave them both a hug. "We need to be going out for the evening. Do your mom a favor and stay inside till we get back."

Buck looked at Miguel, "Remember when we stayed at your cousin's hotel and what happened there?" Miguel nodded that he remembered. Buck continued, "Same situation, different place."

"Anything I can do to help?" Miguel asked.

"Just watch out for the kids and take care of them," Buck replied.

"Will do and be careful out there."

After another hug from Rachael they left the house, got in their truck, and headed towards the Strip.

When they reached the Strip, they parked at Caesar's Palace and started walking the Strip. Buck walked in front of Rachael so as to look like he was alone looking for a good time. Rachael was security for his six-position, watching out for him and looking around as well. After walking for about a quarter mile, Buck hadn't seen or come across any of the working girls.

He looked at Rachael, "I thought that, with me

being so handsome, they would flock to me."

"Truth hurts, don't it?"

Buck looked at her as she smiled. "Ouch, that hurt."

"It'll hurt worse if you don't straighten up here quickly."

"Yes, ma'am." Buck replied, saluting.

"That's better."

They headed into the Mirage Hotel casino and went into the Stack Bar, sat down at the bar, and ordered two Shirley Temples. They sat there, watching, and waiting. Rachael got up from the bar. "I've got to go powder my nose. I'll be right back, and don't you go anywhere."

As she walked away, Buck was sitting there thinking about all that had happened since they got to Vegas. As he was lost in thought, a young lady came over and sat down next to him. At first, Buck didn't pay any attention to her, but catching the scent of her perfume, he looked up. As he looked up, she said, "Care to buy me a drink?"

Buck, thinking this might be one of the girls that belonged to Mako, asked, "What'll you have, Blondie?"

"I'll have a rum and coke, if you don't mind," she replied.

Buck motioned to the bartender and he

delivered a rum and coke to the blonde. By now Rachael was walking back from the restroom and saw what was going on and sat a little further down from them at the bar, watching. When Buck saw Rachael, he was ready to start the play, "What's a nice girl like you doing in a place like this?"

The blonde laughed. "I haven't heard that line since I left home."

"You mean it's not original?" Buck smiled.

"I think I like you." Looking around the bar, she asked, "Do you want to go somewhere more private?"

Buck looked at her. "Depends; what do you have in mind, Blondie?"

"First of all, my name is Veronica and I'm from Los Angeles, and the blond hair is dyed."

"Sorry about that; I always heard blondes have more fun."

"So, did I."

They both laughed and got up from the bar and headed out the door. Rachael was following not too far behind them as they made their way down the Strip. As Buck and Veronica were walking, Buck asked, "Where would you like to go?"

"Oh, not too far, just over there," pointing with her finger to the car lot.

As they continued to walk in that direction, Buck realized it was a trap to take his money and leave him beat up and hurting on the ground.

"Which car is yours?" Buck asked.

"Just over there in the back corner; see, it's the blue convertible," Veronica said.

"I see it; it looks pretty dark over there in the corner," Buck said.

"Are you afraid of the dark--a big man like you?" Veronica laughed.

Buck smiled, "I'm not afraid of anything."

Veronica grabbed Buck's hand and led him to the car. "Come on, there's nobody here but us."

Buck kept following Veronica to the car and saw the man come out of the shadows. Buck stopped and, as the man came forward, caught him with a chop to the neck, which laid the man out on the ground. A second man Buck didn't see blindsided him with a punch to his kidneys. Buck went down and, turning, nailed the guy in the groin, hitting him with his fist. The man went down and was backing up when Buck got up and slammed his face into the side of a car. Breaking the man's nose and knocking a few teeth out in the process, Buck turned around and saw Veronica starting to run. Rachael grabbed her by the hair and threw her to the ground, pointing her gun at Veronica. "Give me a reason to shoot you in the face."

Veronica stopped trying to get away and just lay there on the ground. She started to yell and Buck came over to where Rachael was standing over Veronica. "You keep yelling, I will kill you myself."

Veronica knew Buck was serious and stopped. Buck pulled her up to her feet and, "Where can I find Mako?"

Veronica looked at him, "You a cop?"

"If I was, you would be going to jail right now."

Veronica thought about it for a moment. "Will you let me go if I tell you?"

"Maybe, maybe not; either way, it's your funeral," Buck replied.

Veronica didn't know what to make of Buck and his partner and wasn't sure if she should answer the questions. At this point, Rachael grabbed her by the neck and started forcing her back to the ground. "All right, all right, I'll tell you. He's working the Mandalay Bay Hotel tonight."

"Do you work for him?" Rachael asked.

"No, I don't; I'm not pretty enough for him," Veronica said.

With that, Buck let her go. "If you're lying, I

will find you again and next time you won't have to worry about being a blonde anymore. Oh, by the way, tell your friends they need to find another line of work. They're not very good at this one anymore."

Veronica made a face at Buck as she walked away, looking for the two guys in the car lot. Buck and Rachael followed her with their eyes as she picked up one of the guys. The guy with the bloody nose and missing teeth staggered, following the other two.

"I hope they've got Obama Care, I have a feeling they're going to need it," Rachael said.

Buck looked at her, smiling, "You know how I love it when you're mean."

The both laughed as they made their way back to their truck.

Arriving at the Mandalay Bay Hotel, they parked in the regular parking area and walked into the lobby of the hotel and started on their way to the Eye Candy Sound Lounge. They found a couple of seats at the bar, sat down, and ordered two more Shirley Temples. After looking around the lounge, Rachael noted that the booths were on the outside of the dance floor and the bar was in the center, next to the dance floor.

"This is a nice place, care to dance?" Buck

asked as he was looking around.

Rachael looked at Buck, "You never told me you knew how to dance."

"That's because I don't know how to dance. I move around the floor like a ruptured duck, feathers everywhere."

"We better not, then. We don't want to attract any attention," +Rachael laughed.

"Especially the feathers." Buck smiled.

They sat there watching the crowd as they came and went. Finally, Buck saw something that caught his eye. Buck saw what looked like a working girl trying to come on to one of the men at the bar. The problem was the man was too drunk to be taken seriously. Buck made eye contact with Rachael and got up and walked over to the couple. He asked if there was anything he could do for the lady. She stopped and looked at him. "I'm looking for a good time and he won't have any of it, and who are you?"

"I'm John and I'm looking for a good time," Buck said.

"My name is Lilly and I'm all yours for a good time, if the price is right," the lady said.

Buck smiled and took her by the arm and they both walked out of the lounge, headed to the front of the hotel.

"Do you have a room here at the hotel?" Lilly

asked.

"No, but I can get one if you like," Buck said.

"That won't be a problem; I've got one here."

"Well, then, lead the way."

Rachael was watching from the front of the lounge and followed them to the third floor. Using another elevator, she was able to stay in the shadows of the rooms and watch as Buck and Lilly went into one of the rooms. Buck made sure the door was ajar for Rachael so that she could come in when it was time.

"How much do you want for having a good time?" Buck asked Lilly.

"You look like you can pay about 100 dollars for some fun."

With that, Rachael came through the door and flashed her badge at Lilly so quickly that she couldn't tell that it was from Arizona. Buck caught Lilly as she was trying to get out of the hotel room.

"You aren't going anywhere. Sit down on the bed and you won't get hurt," Buck said.

"What kind of deal is this; are you a cop?" Lilly asked.

"Yes, we are cops, and we're not interested in busting you. We want some information."

"What kind of information do you want from me?"

"We want to know where Mako is," Rachael said.

"I don't know a Mako."

Rachael pulled her gun out and loaded a bullet into the chamber, and as she did so, she said, "I believe you do. It's the only deal you're going to get tonight. Now, where can we find Mako?"

Lilly turned white as a sheet and started to stammer. "Okay, Okay, I know who he is."

"Now that's better; answer the lady before she shoots you," Buck said.

"I don't know where he is right now. We don't see him until morning when he picks us up after we're finished working. All I know is he drives a black BMW with a license plate that reads 'One and Only' on it," Lilly said.

"Where does he hang out when he's not doing business?" asked Buck.

"He likes the Ruby Club on Las Vegas Boulevard."

Buck handed her a fifty-dollar bill, "At least, it wasn't a complete waste of time."

Lilly took the money and left the hotel room in a hurry.

"I wonder if she'll put that towards paying off her college loans?" Rachael asked.

Buck and Rachael left the room and went back

down the elevator to go to their truck. Once inside the truck, they started down the Strip, driving both ways, looking for a black Beemer with personalized license plates. Around sunup they headed to the Ruby Club and sat in the parking lot for a while, watching the cars going in and out. After an hour of watching and not seeing the black Beemer, they left and found a Denny's restaurant and stopped there to have breakfast.

When they got back to Gared's place, it was about 9:00 am. They said their hello's and headed off to the bedroom to get some sleep. Just before dozing off Miguel came in. "Where were you guys last night?"

"We went out on the town last night to see the sights," Rachael answered.

Buck nodded in agreement with what Rachael had said, adding, "Las Vegas is really pretty at night when it's all lit up, isn't it?"

"Please, no more questions, we've been up all night and we need to get some sleep, so off you go," Rachael said.

Miguel looked at both of them and said nothing and walked out of the room. Buck looked at Rachael. "I know he doesn't believe us, but its better this way, I think." With that, they lay down and were out in seconds.

Chapter IV

Later that day when they woke up, Buck and Rachael walked into the kitchen to get some coffee. Tina was there washing dishes, "Hello, how are you two doing this fine day?"

"You know what they say about Vegas? What goes on in Vegas stays in Vegas," Buck said, smiling.

Tina laughed. "You are something else, aren't you?"

"You don't know the half of it," Rachael said.

"Oh, I almost forgot to tell you, you need to call the FBI again. Here is their number," Tina said.

Buck looked at Rachael, "I'll take care of it," Rachael said as she got up to leave the kitchen.

She went into the den and dialed the number to the FBI office. Waiting for the secretary to pick up the phone, Rachael sat there sipping her coffee. After the fifth ring, Sherron still hadn't answered the phone. She hung up and walked back to the kitchen and sat down. Buck could see that something was wrong and asked her,

"What's up?"

"Nobody picked up the phone when I called the office," Rachael told Buck.

Buck thought that was strange. "Maybe we need to go down there and check it out. It's probably nothing, but we'll go check it out anyway."

As they drove down to the Las Vegas Federal Building, Buck asked Rachael, "Is it normal for the office to be empty during working hours?"

Rachael shook her head no. "And that's what has me worried about it."

When they walked into the office, the door was unlocked. As they carefully made their way inside to Warren's office, they found that it had been ransacked. The files were all over the floor and Warren's desk was turned over on its back. Buck checked the phone to see if it was still working. It wasn't, and as he pulled on the phone cord, he could see that it had been cut.

Rachael called out to Buck, "Come quick!"

There on the floor in the other room was Sherron. Buck knelt down to see if she was alive, and after checking her pulse, he was surprised that she was.

"Call 911 now!" Buck told Rachael.

The ambulance and the E.M.T.s both arrived in about five minutes. The E.M.T.s had Sherron lying on the gurney and out the door and in the ambulance in less time than it took them to get there.

As the ambulance left to go to the hospital, one of the E.M.T.s said to Buck and Rachael, "It's a good thing you called when you did; otherwise, she would have died."

"What happened to her?" Buck asked the medic.

"Someone tried to kill her with some kind of blunt object to the head."

"What do you think of putting a guard on the secretary, just in case they try again?" Rachael asked.

"Yes, but who can we get to do this, seeing as how were not from around here?" asked Buck.

After the E.M.T.s left, Rachael asked Buck, as she looked at the mess in the office, "Should we call our friends in Washington?"

Buck nodded. "I think we'd better."

Rachael reached Linda on the phone through her personal number. Linda was surprised to hear from her. "What's going on down there in Arizona?"

"I've got bad news for you. First of all, we're in Vegas at the FBI office and none of your agents are here. We just found the secretary half dead on the floor. The office looks like a tornado went through it, and it looks like whoever did this was looking for something in the filing cabinets."

"Are you guys all right? What are you doing in Las Vegas?"

Linda listened without interrupting while Rachael explained why they were there. "Let me call you back; I've got to talk to Evans about this. Is this your cell phone number that you're calling from?" Linda asked.

"Yes, it is."

"Good, I'll call you back shortly and I'll get a security team to the hospital for the secretary."

With that, the phone went dead. Rachael closed her cell phone and put it away for the moment. Buck was talking to the Metro officers, who responded when the ambulance was called. They took his report, "We'll be in touch if we have any more questions, and just as a matter of courtesy, please let us know if you leave town."

Buck nodded his head. "Not a problem; we'll be here in town for a while."

After the Metro officers left, Buck went to where Rachael was standing in front of Warren's office door.

"A penny for your thoughts."

"What were they looking for?" Rachael asked as she smiled at Buck's comment.

"What?" said Buck.

"Why would they risk coming into the FBI's office and ransack it; why would they risk it all and for what?"

Buck thought about the question and suddenly the light came on. "Maybe they were looking for pictures, our pictures."

"We need to go back to the house and check on the kids."

Buck and Rachael went to their truck, where they found a note on the windshield. Buck picked it up and read it, then gave the note to Rachael, who in turn read it. She started to tear up and got angry. "Somebody knows where we are staying, and now they know where the kids are."

They quickly drove to Gared and Tina's house and went inside, searching each room with their guns drawn and yelling "clear" as they exited each room. When they reached the kitchen, they found Tina making dinner and watching TV. She looked up, "Hi guys; you're home early."

"Where are the kids?" Rachael asked excitedly.

Tina looked at them and laughed, "You're joking, aren't you? You called them to meet you at the college, didn't you?"

"No, we didn't," replied Buck.

Buck had Rachael call the police and alert them to the situation about the kids being chased by Ice Man and Mako's goons. Metro said they would contact the campus police and put a BOLO (Be on the Look Out) on them.

Tina looked worried. "That wasn't you that called on the phone?"

Rachael shook her head no. "Did Tim go with them?"

"No, he's still upstairs in bed," Tina replied.

Buck was listening to all of the conversation. "That's good. Don't let anyone into the house unless you know them, even if it's the police. Do you understand what I'm telling you?"

"Yes, but I don't understand what's going on," Tina replied.

Rachael told Tina about what they had found at the FBI office earlier that day and how the pictures that Tim and Jennifer had taken were missing. "Evidently, because of the break-in, they now have your phone number and address. That's how they knew where to call the kids. Now the kids might be in danger from the goons working for Ice Man and Mako."

Tina looked at both of them, almost in tears, "What do you want me to do?"

"Stay inside and keep an eye on Tim, and do what Buck just told you to do," Rachael replied.

After checking on Tim, Buck and Rachael got into their truck and made their way to the college. As they were driving to the college, Rachael's cell phone rang, she answered, "Hello."

"Hello, Rachael, and how are you this fine day?" The voice on the other end said.

"Who is this, and what do you want?"

"I want the negatives of the pictures you had processed, and I'll let the kids go. Without the negatives, no kids; do you understand?" the voice said.

"Yes, how do I know you have the kids?" Rachael asked.

After a pause of a few seconds, the voice of Marissa came on the line. "Hello."

"Are you all right?" asked Rachael.

"Yes, we're fine; is Miguel with you?"

At that point, the voice of the man came back on. "There's your proof. We'll be in contact with you soon to set up the meet."

The phone went dead. Rachael looked at Buck, "They've only got the girls; Miguel isn't with them."

Buck sat thinking as he was driving. "I wonder where he is?"

As they continued driving to the college, Buck had an idea. "Knowing our son, I wonder if he followed them, staying out of sight, and hoping for a chance to get them out of the jam they're in."

"I hope you're right."

When they got to the college, they stopped in at the campus police office and went in to talk to the chief. After identifying themselves and why they were there the police chief said, "I'm sorry, we looked all over the campus and couldn't find hide nor hair of the kids. If they wanted to hide on this campus, they could, and we wouldn't be able to find them, no matter how hard we looked."

Buck and Rachael agreed with him and thanked him for trying to find them. After leaving the office Rachael said, "What do we do now?"

Buck looked at her, "What can we do. We wait for the phone call and hope that Miguel contacts us soon."

While they waited for the phone call, they went down to the Strip and looked for the black Beemer, hoping they would get lucky in finding Mako. When the phone rang again, Rachael picked it up and answered it. This time, it was Evans on the line, "Are you guys all right?"

Rachael told him of the current situation with the kids and how the pictures of the drug drop were missing. "We're currently driving the Strip, looking for a pimp named Mako, who was in the pictures."

After hearing Rachael's report Evans replied, "We are en-route to Vegas and should be there in about an hour. Can we meet you at the FBI office?"

"Yes, that would be fine; we'll meet you there in about two hours."

"Fine; we'll see you then."

As they cruised the Strip for about an hour, nothing came up, even with checking the Ruby Club. Rachael was getting nervous and Buck was just plain mad and thinking out loud, "We need to get over to the FBI office now."

When they arrived at the federal building, they went into the FBI office and met with the federal police. They showed them their own credentials from Arizona. One of the federal police officers, recognizing them, allowed them inside the office. Buck and Rachael started going through the mess of papers and files that were on the floor, looking for any clues that would help them find where the kids had been taken.

After 30 minutes of searching the files in both rooms, Evans and Linda showed up in the office. After the customary hugs and handshakes, the four of them went into Warren's office, where the cleanup crew had set the desk and chairs back into their regular places. As they sat down and tried to sort out the mess, Buck told Evans and Linda one more time about Tim and Jennifer's experience with the plane landing in the desert, the offloading of drugs into a van, and almost being caught by the bad guys.

"What happened to the pictures?" Evans asked.

"We had them developed and brought them here to Warren. He handed them off to Jenkins to do a follow-up on the license plate and tail number on the plane and also to do a facial recognition on the people in the photos," Rachael said.

Buck continued, "The facial recognition got hits on two of the faces and were able to identify one as Ice Man and the other as Mako. Ice man is the biggest drug dealer here in Vegas, and Mako is the pimp that works the Strip area. Mako is who we were after the other night. We were able to find out that he drives a black BMW with a license plate that reads "One and Only" on it. We know he frequents the Ruby Club on Las Vegas Boulevard, and that's all we know right now."

"How much does Warren know about Mako and this car that he drives?" asked Evans.

"We were going to tell him when we met again but never got the chance to do so," replied Buck.

Linda looked at both Rachael and Buck and could tell they were tired. "When was the last time you guys slept really well?"

"Before we left Arizona; since then, we have been searching for Mako pretty much every night," Buck said.

"Buck and I think they ransacked the office for the pictures we left with Warren and what other information they had about the kids and where they were staying," Rachael said.

"We plan on doing an inventory and we'll let you know what we find is missing. Until then, go look for your son and we'll check on the secretary to see if she knows who did this. We will be staying at one of the hotels off the Strip. We'll let you know which one when we find it ourselves," Evans replied.

"I don't know if you aware of this or not, the secretary, Sherron, has been working here for the FBI in this office for over seven years now. Evidently, she was instrumental in solving some of the cases dealing with interstate theft and white slavery issues a while back. She also pointed out discrepancies when typing the transcripts for the agents, before Warren was transferred here. If anybody knows what's going on in this office, she would know all about it. It's lucky for her and us that she survived the assault, when they came in to get the pictures of the drug drop," Linda said.

"Yes, very lucky indeed," Rachael replied.

"You won't believe how lucky she is, after we posted a guard outside her hospital room, later that day two men showed up asking about Sherron and what room she was in. When the nurse refused to tell them, they got belligerent with her. The security guard, seeing the commotion, called for backup and just in time. The extra security guard showed up along with the police, and arrested the two men who were carrying guns who were later identified as soldiers for Iceman."

Both Buck and Rachael stood there for a moment thinking how all of this was turning all the wrong way for everybody involved. Buck looked at Evans with a dark look in his eyes, "We would like to stay on top of trying to find Mako. Right now, he is our only lead to who may know where to find the kids."

"Go for it. If you find him, let us know and we'll go from there," Evans said.

"Will do," said Buck.

With that, Buck and Rachael went to their

truck and headed back to Gared and Tina's house.

When they arrived, they went up to the house and Tina was waiting at the door, having heard them drive up. "Any news about the kids?"

"We got a call from them about a swap for the pictures. We're still waiting for the phone call to set up the meeting place for the swap," Buck said.

"How's Tim doing?" Rachael asked.

"He's doing better now," Tina replied.

Buck and Rachael decided to go upstairs to talk to Tim about where the kids liked to hang out while at school. When they opened the door, Tim was getting dressed to go outside. Buck looked at him. "Now where do you think you're going?"

"I got them into this mess; I'm going to find them and make it right," Tim replied, feeling a little lightheaded.

Buck and Rachael looked at each other and smiled. Buck continued, "We appreciate your willingness to help, but you're our key witness and you've got to stay here and be safe so you can testify against these people when it comes time."

Tim looked up with tears in his eyes, "But I want to help find them. It's my fault they've been taken."

Tina came in the room and, seeing that Tim was getting dressed to go, "Tim I need you here to help me in case they call here."

Tim tried standing up and almost fell over; luckily, Buck caught him before he hit the floor. He picked Tim up and put him back in bed and said to the boy, "You've done your part; let us help you with the rest of it now. We'll find them one way or another."

Tim, still feeling weak, lay back down on the bed and was out again.

"It would probably be a good idea to have the doctor come and take a look at him again," said Buck.

Tina looked at both Buck and Rachael. "Your world is so different from mine, and I know you'll find them; and when you do, please bring them home safely. As far as the men that did this to Tim, show no mercy to them."

Buck and Rachael looked at her and seeing that she meant every word said, "That won't be a problem; they threatened our son, too."

As they left the house one more time and headed to the truck, Rachael looked at Buck, "How do we find Miguel?"

"I don't rightly know," Buck said, looking at Rachael. "Hopefully, he'll call us first."

Arriving at the Ruby Club, Buck and Rachael sat in the truck and waited, hoping that the black BMW would drive into the parking lot.

Chapter V

Mako was driving his Beemer down Lake Mead Boulevard heading out to Lake Mead to go swimming with some of his working girls. This was their day off for working the Strip last night. As far as pimps go he was better than most. He treated his girls better than the other pimps that worked in Vegas, simply because he would only beat them when it was necessary, not all of the time. When they did good he would treat them to a holiday, like going to the lake or giving them the night off to rest and do want they wanted to do.

Mako started out working the side streets near the Strip and from there he worked his way to the Strip by beating out his competition. He did this with better looking girls and better prices for them, and if necessary killing the competitors and taking over that part of the street. He was ruthless but only when it served him to do so. He was a business man first and foremost and his business was giving pleasure to the pleasure seekers at a fair price for Vegas. He had thought about setting up a ranch like the ones they had in Nye County but the sheriff's department monitored all of the action that occurred in the brothel. Even though it was considered illegal in Clark County the money was here simply because the gambling was here. Plus driving to the legal places was too far to drive for most of the men. Hence, the best money was here on the streets in Las Vegas.

The girls he used were only the pretty ones he had found around the bus depot, looking lost and running from the problems they had left behind. Most of the girls were looking for fame and fortune just like those that went to be a movie star in Hollywood. He would take them in and care for them until they were ready to work doing tricks. The older girls, who were working for him, would take the new ones under their wings, and set them up working on the Strip. They would explain the basics of the business to them until they were able to work it on their own. When they were able to do this the girls would report directly to Mako handing their money over to him. Otherwise the older girls would collect the money and turn it over to Mako.

Mako had decided to branch out into the drug scene, by not only providing girls, but drugs as well to the customers, in a sense a one-stop shop. For this one reason, he wanted to work with Ice Man who was the main supplier for the drugs in the city. Ice man was a dangerous man and he understood that you didn't cross him on the money or the drugs. For Mako it was a marriage of necessity for the time being. Least wise, until the right opportunity presented itself to him. The story is, Ice Man once killed a dealer for trying to short change him. The police found the drug dealers body in a shallow grave out in the desert next to a new housing subdivision. Mako dealt with Ice Man only when he needed to, not because he was afraid of him, but because the man was an animal in his eyes and he didn't consider himself in the same light as Ice Man.

The night he went with Ice Man to get the drugs off the plane, out in the desert near Pahrump, he went as a guest. Ice Man wanted to show Mako his operation for the drug running in Nevada. Needless to say, you didn't tell Ice Man no, when he asked you to go, you went. After assisting in the setup of the flares for the makeshift landing Strip, they waited for the plane to show. It was 9:30 pm when the plane flew over; it was a Cessna 340, a five passenger aircraft which could haul approximately two thousand pounds of cargo with a flying distance of 1400 nautical miles. The plane could fly from California and back on one tank of gas in one night. Ice Man's pickup vehicles would have a team of men to unload the cargo in a short time. The plane would be airborne and on its way back to California inside 20 minutes without anybody aware of what took place. Mako thought how sweet it would be to own an airplane like that for his own use, maybe someday.

When the drugs were loaded onto the vehicles they would get moving down highway 95. The vehicle would drive by the Nevada test site and Old Indian Springs Air Force base back to Las Vegas to drop off the drugs at a warehouse in West Las Vegas Industrial Park. There the drugs would be worked until they were ready for distribution along the street corners of Las Vegas. Some of the kilos would be sent to Reno for distribution there, as well. Mako thought to himself, when he saw the money in the sale of drugs, he wanted to be a part of that as well as the prostitution racket. The big secret for drug selling was to never get hooked on what you sold. Mako understood that as well when it came to the working girls, never let yourself fall for any of them, they could be your downfall in this business. Treat them all the same way, no favorites, no special anything to anyone of them. That was good business sense all the way around.

When Mako was dropped off from the excursion in the desert he let Ice Man know he wanted in on the action. Ice Man said he would think about it and be in touch with him. With that, Mako was waiting to see what would happen. In the meantime, he was on his way to Lake Mead with some of his girls looking to have a good time playing in the water. Treating the girls to a big dinner afterwards, and spending money on them for clothes and anything they wanted that night. Tomorrow would be another day working the Strip until the next day off.

Mako showed the girls a good time and when it was time to go home most of the girls were ready to go. Having had fun at Lake Mead, shopping at the mall, and eating, they were tired and ready to go home to sleep. Mako had a house in which the girls called home. It was a six thousand square foot house with eight bedrooms and three baths in it. Each of the girls shared a room with one other girl and if the shifts were right the girls would never run into each other except maybe in the mornings. The house overlooked Las Vegas valley and off in the distance you could see Red Rocks from the balcony as well as the Strip. It was situated near Sunrise Mountain actually, at the base of the mountain.

The girls would be dropped off at 7:30 pm at a specified location and picked up at 8:00 am the following morning at the same place where they had been dropped off. Mako would do the delivery and the pickups himself that way there was no middle man. He would collect the money and do the counting himself with a money machine to assist him. When the conventions were in town the money was good and when it was just the local crowd business was slower. Ebb and flow in all things when it came to the Las Vegas Strip. The girls would get money enough to keep them working there, but not as much as Mako.

Mako was originally from New Jersey and was working as a card dealer in one of the casinos. The hours and money were not enough for his tastes in life and he wanted more of the good life. He headed out to Vegas to make it rich. He found the same situation in Vegas as he had experienced in New Jersey. Tiring of this, he started off with a couple girls hustling them to make money and went from there, getting more girls along the way. The nickname, Mako, came about from his pearly white teeth, the Corvette Stingray he drove, and the knife he used when it was necessary. He didn't mind the nickname, in fact, it bolstered his image around town and that was always good for his line of business. In fact, Mako was on top of his game and it was only going to get better from here.

As Mako pulled into the Ruby Club he got out of his BMW and started to walk into the club. Buck and Rachael were watching from across the street when he pulled into the parking lot. When Buck got ready to get out of the truck to go after Mako, Rachael put her hand on his arm, "Wait let's get him on the way out of the club. Besides it's almost dark, it's better for us not to have any witnesses."

Buck settled back into his seat and waited for the darkness. He checked his watch and it read 8:00 pm. Mako had just dropped off the girls to work the Strip and was coming to the Ruby Club to kill some time before going back to the house. At about 11:00 pm, Rachael nudged Buck, who had fallen asleep, "There he is."

Buck got out of the truck and walked over to Mako and asked for a light for his cigarette. Mako didn't smoke so he told Buck, "I don't smoke but you can get some matches inside," pointing to the club.

At that time, Buck hit him right in the stomach and Mako went down but came back up with his knife and Buck jumped back as Mako made a thrust at him. Buck caught his arm and snapped it by twisting it backwards at the elbow. Mako let out a scream of pain and dropped the knife on the ground. By now, Rachael brought the truck over and help Buck throw Mako in the back of it. Mako, still holding his broken arm, cried out every time he moved in the back of the truck. Buck and Rachael drove out of town towards Beatty on route 95 and just passed Lathrop Wells they took a right on a dirt road out into the desert. Making sure they were alone and far enough off the main route, they stopped the truck and pulled Mako out of the back of the truck and threw him on the ground. As he lay there Buck put his foot on the broken arm which made Mako scream in pain.

Buck took his foot off, "Now that I got your attention, we have a few questions for you and if we think you're lying I'll break your other arm."

Mako, starting to go into shock from the pain fought to regain his thoughts, "Who are you and what do you want from me?"

"We are concerned parents and are worried about the negative influence you have on our children," Rachael replied.

Mako didn't understand what she was talking about. "What?"

This time Rachael bent down with the barrel of her gun under his chin, "We need to know where we can find Ice Man."

Mako looked up at her surprised. "If I tell you he'll kill me for sure, there's no way I'm telling you that."

Rachael fired her gun putting the bullet into Mako's knee cap. Mako let out another scream and yelled, cussing her out for shooting him in the leg. Rachael looked at Mako, bleeding from the knee and trying to hold his arm from hurting any more than it did.

"We want to know where we can find Ice Man. Look at it this way, you can still survive the night if you tell us," Rachael said.

By now, Mako was fading in and out of consciousness, and he knew he wouldn't make it unless he told them what they wanted to know.

"Alright, I'll tell you. He's at Spring Valley, he has a warehouse there for his operation."

Buck leaned over and asked, "What part of spring Valley?"

"Off of Flamingo Road and Raven Wood Drive," Mako groaned.

Buck and Rachael got into their truck and started to drive off. Mako yelled, "What about me?"

Buck looked at him, "Yes what about you?" and drove off leaving him there to make his way back to Vegas.

With the new information Buck and Rachael headed back to Vegas looking for Ice Man's place.

Chapter VI

Ice Man, aka, Mr. Bronson, aka, Mr. Smith, was from California, Fresno California to be exact. He was a drug pusher that started in Fresno and ended up in Las Vegas, making money hand over fist working the streets and the stars in Las Vegas. He was known as a big man in the world of Las Vegas and had connections with the syndicate operating in Las Vegas with a percentage of his drug profits going directly to the syndicate. With a mutual agreement between the syndicate and Ice Man, he was protected from the others who wanted to come in and set up their own drug operations in Vegas. The syndicate handled the murders and payoffs, thereby, Ice Man's hands were always clean from the dirt in Vegas. In the cases where he was involved, he took great pleasure in getting rid of his competition. In fact, to him it was fun to see the competition beg for their lives and start crying when they knew he was going to kill them. Ice Man was ruthless and his way of getting rid of the competition was to destroy it, if it couldn't be bought off he would figure a way to get rid of it. The desert was a great place to hide anything or anybody. All you had to do is find a quiet place in the middle of nowhere and bring a shovel and start digging.

The night he had Mako with him was to show off part of his drug business, it was more of a show and tell that he wanted Mako to see. So Mako would know that he had the connections for the drugs and also the means to carry it out. While one team was downloading the drugs from the plane, he was also burying one of his competitors. Mako pretended not to notice but Ice Man wanted to make sure the point was made real clear. This was about the consequences of double crossing him, and his way of handling it. Ice Man stood there laughing as the body was thrown into a shallow grave and covered up. When you looked into Ice Man's eyes it was like looking into hell, there was no life or feelings in his eyes, at all. He had prided himself in being a killer, this was something he had learned when he lived in Fresno dealing with the gangs there. No emotions, no feeling, when it came to his wants and needs, it was all business. There was no room for compassion for anyone. This was the downfall of his mentor in the drug business. The mentor had taken a liking to Ice Man and took him under his wing to teach him about his business. Ice Man pretended to care about the mentor in order to kill him and take over his drug business. The look of surprise on the mentor's face as he lay there dying with Ice Man smiling at him, was the only mistake his mentor had made and he paid dearly for it. But that was years before he came to Vegas. Ice Man had plans of expanding his drug business, and Vegas was the jewel in the crown for money and connections. After getting rid of the competition in Vegas, he took over and actually started showing a profit in the drug trade. Once the syndicate saw this, they approached him with the deal of working together, and from there it was a profitable arrangement between the two of them.

After he found out that pictures had been taken of him out in the desert, he knew that the pictures and the picture takers had to be found. It was pure luck that one of his men saw the flash from the cell phone camera that night. After the man chased after the two people, he was able to get the license plate and make and model of the car. It was a simple check on the license plate at one of the DMV's from one of his so-called friends that worked there to find out the name and address to the owner of the car. It was only a matter of time to track Tim and Jennifer down and find their place.

Ice Man knew that the pictures would be enough to put him away for a long time in prison and he couldn't risk it. Tim and Jennifer had to be found and the threat had to be terminated, including anyone that they had told about what they saw in the desert that night. The one person they started following was a Spanish looking guy that Tim had hung out with. Ice Man didn't know his name, all he knew was, he couldn't take the chance of this kid staying alive. Ice Man had the kid followed, trying to tie up the loose ends and make sure his secret in the desert remained a secret. The problem was his men were seen and the boy was able to get away from them by creating a disturbance in the casino.

His men had found Tim and while they were in the process of extracting information from Tim he was able to get away from them. Ice Man let him get away in order to catch them all in one place. It almost worked when they were able to track Tim and Jennifer to the Spanish kid's place. The one thing they hadn't counted on was their slipping away in the cover of darkness. The only thing they had to go on was trying to locate them again through their cell phones, and their inside source from the FBI. Once the pictures turned up at the FBI office, Ice Man knew he had to act fast or it was all over for him. This was getting out of hand for the Ice Man and he had to do something. His source told him about the phone number and taking a chance called the number thinking this would be the way to catch them all at once. Having the kids meet him at the college was the answer. The problem was when the kids got there the Spanish kid had to go to one of his professors to explain why he and his girlfriend had missed his class. Letting the boy go while getting the girls was good enough for the Ice Man's men, the girls could be used to flush out Tim and the photo negatives. When the boy came back and saw that the girls were gone he went into hiding. Miguel saw the girls being taken away by the two men but couldn't do anything to stop it. He had tried to follow the girls but somehow the two men lost the boy in their getaway.

Miguel knew if he went back to the house he was staying at, the owners could get hurt or worse. So, he took off on his own to find the place the two men took the girls. Not knowing where to go, he headed in the same direction the car had taken. As he made his way down the street he wished he had his cell phone to call his parents, and or Tina and Gared, to let them know where he was. Seeing some kids standing on the corner of the street, Miguel asked if he could use one of their cell phones to call his parents. At first the kids were leery but he told them that he wasn't trying to do anything and that it was an emergency. Calling Buck and Rachael and finally getting through was a relief for all concerned. Rachael answered the phone, "Hello, who is this?"

"It's Miguel."

"Oh, thank goodness, where are you?"

"I'm at the corner of Sahara and Lake Mead Boulevard."

"Stay there and we'll come get you."

"Mom they took the girls, what are we going to do now?"

"We know Miguel, and were going to get them back as soon as we can. Stay there, try not to worry. We're coming to get you."

In about 15 minutes, Buck and Rachael showed up to get Miguel. Rachael got out of the truck and ran over and gave him a hug and then started to scold him for going off without checking with them first. All Miguel could do was stand there and let her get it out of her system. After the scolding, she hugged him again and was crying when they both got into the truck. Buck looked at him, "Are you all right boy?"

"Yes sir, I am, but they got the girls."

"I know they do, but we need to get you back to the house right now."

Miguel started to say something then thought better of it, and was silent the rest of the trip back to the house. Tina was happy to see that Miguel was alright and that Buck and Rachael had found him. Tina kept asking about the girls, but getting no answer, she stopped asking realizing it was not a good situation for the girls or for Buck and Rachael. Buck and Rachael didn't say anything about Mako or for the matter, about having an idea where they could be.

It took all night for Mako to crawl to the highway and get picked up by a good Samaritan and be taken to a Las Vegas hospital. The prognosis from the doctor was that he would walk again, but with a limp. His arm was in a cast as he lay in the bed. Some of his working girls came by to check on him and see how he was doing. All Mako could think of was that these two people, who had kidnapped him and left him in the desert, were going to pay for what they had done to him.

Mako, looking at his girls, asked, "Do you have a phone I can use?" One of the girls handed her phone to him.

Mako made the call to Ice Man. "Ice Man we got a problem."

"What kind of problem do you have that affects me?" Ice man said.

"Two people, a man and a woman, took me out into the desert and wanted to know where they could find you."

"What did you tell them?"

Mako was hesitant to say the next part. "After the women shot me in the kneecap I told them where to find you."

This upset Ice Man. "You better be glad you're in the hospital already or I would put you there myself."

"What are you going to do now?"

"Don't you worry about it, I'll take care of it myself."

Mako hung up the phone, thinking to himself, for the first time I'm glad I'm in the hospital.

Ice Man wondered who these two people were that were asking for him and what they wanted. He called his informant from the FBI office, "Who are these two people and what do they want?"

"If it's who I think it is you want nothing to

do with them. They 're both cops and the female used to be an FBI agent," the informant replied.

Ice man thought about what the informant had told him for a moment, "Do you know where I can find them?"

"They never told me."

"I've got my own problems right now, two high powered agents from Washington are here to investigate what happened in my office when you came in and got the pictures."

Ice Man calmly told him, "Handle it, that's what I'm paying you for right?"

"I'm not sure I can at this point."

"You better, or I'll take care of you myself."

"Okay, I will," said the informant, realizing that his life was on the line.

Ice Man hung up the phone, and looked at the two girls, and wondered if they were what the two-people wanted. He laughed to himself saying two can play at this game.

Ice Man called his liaison to the syndicate, "I need to meet with Frankie today."

The man on the other end said, "Wait a minute I'll check."

A moment later the man said, "How about 9:30 tonight same place as usual."

"That would be fine," Ice Man replied.

In the meantime, Ice Man decided to move the

girls to a safer place away from his base of operations. He had his men take the girls up to his house in the canyon at Mount Charleston. His men could see from there who was coming and going from his house up there. When Marissa and Jennifer were brought from the locked room he had them in, the look of fear was in their eyes. He could tell they were scared but both of them wouldn't let it out. The two girls were then blindfolded and put in the back of the van, they were tied together and their mouths were taped over so they couldn't scream for help. It was an hour to get to Ice Man's house near Mount Charleston. Once there, the men left the blindfolds on them as well as the tape covering their mouths. One of the men contacted Ice Man to let him know that they had arrived at his house without being followed.

Ice Man smiled and said to himself, "Now try and find the girls, Mr. and Mrs. FBI."

Ice Man hung up the phone and then speaking to his men said, "We may be having some company coming over soon." His men started to check their weapons and position themselves to set up a defense inside the building.

Buck and Rachael talked to Miguel alone in the den. "We need you to stay here and keep an eye on Tim."

"What about the girls?" Miguel replied.

"We have an Idea where they're at, but we got to go now, to get them back. Promise you'll stay here until we get back," Buck said.

Miguel didn't like it, but he knew if anybody could get them it would be his parents. "I promise," Miguel replied.

Buck called Evans, "We have an idea where the girls might be. According to our sources they may be in a warehouse on Flamingo Road and Raven Wood Drive."

"How do you want to handle it?" Evans asked.

"Let us check it out first and we'll give you call when we're ready to take it."

"You know you're on your own with this? Until we find the mole here, we can't afford to let anyone know what you're doing."

"That won't be a problem, with Rachael, I'm sure we can take care of this ourselves."

"Oh, one more thing one of the bad guy pimps is in the hospital and he's been shot in the leg and has a broken arm. Do you guys have any idea about this pimp and what happened to him?"

Buck smiled, "No, not a clue, but I'll ask Rachael maybe she knows something about it."

Evans chuckled, "Maybe she does," and hung up the phone.

Buck looked at Rachael, "Mako made it back to civilization and is in the hospital."

"Oh joy, maybe we need to go see him again when this is all done," Rachael replied.

"Maybe sooner than later."

Buck and Rachael arrived at the warehouses on Flamingo and Raven Wood and sat there for about an hour trying to figure which one of the warehouses to go check out.

Buck looked at Rachael, "You know they're probably waiting for us in there, don't you think?"

"We wouldn't want to disappoint them now, would we? How do you want to handle this?"

"First of all, we really don't know which one of these warehouses they're in. Secondly, we don't know what the layout is inside, either."

"How about we go look inside each one of the warehouses and see if they are connected to each other."

"What a brilliant idea!"

About the time they were trying to determine which to check first, a car drove up and the garage door opened. A man carrying a gun, came out to check the car and to let him in. After the car passed the garage door closed and everything was quiet again. Rachael looked at Buck, "I think it's that one."

"What makes you say that?" Buck asked.

"It's obvious that the man had a gun in his coat."

"How could you tell from here?"

Rachael smiled, "Remember I'm an FBI trained person."

"I bet your fun at the parties. Let's go check out the building and see if there is another way in."

Rachael and Buck, making sure they had the tape and plastic tie wraps, walked around the building looking for another entrance. They found one on the backside, adjacent to the warehouse they wanted. Rachael was able to open the door by picking the lock. Once inside they used their flashlights to look around. Buck looked up and noticed a skylight and pointed it out to Rachael. They started looking for a ladder that would lead them to the skylight. It took about ten minutes of searching before they found a ladder attached to the wall. After climbing it they found a small door that led to the adjacent warehouse. Climbing through the door and onto the other side, they could see where the enforcers were hiding and where the main office was for Ice Man. They carefully climbed down the ladder to get inside the building and as they scouted the area inside the warehouse, they noticed that there was another room that was guarded by one man. The van they had been looking for wasn't there, however, the car that went in earlier that evening was still there. Rachael got the license plate number and wrote it down for future reference and put it in her pocket.

Buck started on one side of the warehouse, while Rachael started on the other side. As they made their way they would subdue the enforcers one by one, securing them with duct tape and plastic tie wraps. Once they made their way throughout the warehouse and disabling Ice Man's men, they ended up at the room where the guard was blocking the door. Buck snuck up on the guy as Rachael made a noise to distract him. Once away from the door, Buck cold cocked him and dragged him off to join the others that were tied and gagged. Rachael picked the lock of the door, and opening it, she saw a stash of drugs inside. And she stood there looking in the room, it was about three quarters full of kilo size bricks of drugs, all nicely wrapped in plastic and ready for delivery to the dealers. Rachael waited for Buck to finish securing the guard, and as she stood there looking at the drugs, she took her knife and started opening the bricks and throwing the drugs on the ground. Buck joined in and pretty soon the room was full of white powder all over the floor. With that done, they dragged the bodies of the enforcers into the room where the drugs had been stored and destroyed and left them in there to be found by Ice Man and his friends. Buck and Rachael left the warehouse the same way they had come in, by climbing the ladder and crossing over into the next warehouse and climbing back down. Once outside, they sat in their car and waited for what would happen next.

Ice Man came down from his office yelling, "Johnny, get my car it's time to go meet Frankie Diamond!"

When Johnny didn't acknowledge his request, he called again. Still no answer from Johnny. This time calling, "Hey Al, where is everybody?"

Still no answer. Ice Man started walking around the warehouse looking for his men. Finding none, he went to check the locked storage room. Finding the door locked he looked down and saw some white powder on the warehouse floor. Pulling out his keys, and unlocking the door, he found his men plus the drugs strewn all over the floor. Realizing that someone had been inside the warehouse destroying all of his drugs, he pulled his gun out and started searching the area. At this point, he started yelling, "Where are you, come and get me!"

Still looking for where they could be hiding, Ice Man and his men, once they had been released from their bindings, checked out the whole building. Buck and Rachael waited patiently in their truck and watched as the garage door opened. Ice Man's men had their guns drawn looking all around for whoever had caught them flat footed. Once the area was deemed secure by his men, the car quickly drove through the door of the warehouse. Buck put the truck into gear and proceeded to follow the car. Following the car, they made their way to a restaurant across the street from the Landmark Hotel called The Alpine Village. Parking across the street, Buck and Rachael watched Ice Man exit his car and walk into the restaurant.

Ice Man could see Frankie sitting by himself with two men watching. When Frankie saw Ice Man, he motioned for him to come over. Frankie looked at him, "You look upset, what's wrong?"

"Somehow, someone got inside the warehouse and destroyed all of the drugs that were ready for shipment. We're talking about a couple million dollars of drugs that are no good anymore," Ice Man told Frankie.

Frankie put down his fork, "You want me to take care of it for you?"

"Yes, but before you do I want to meet whoever it is that did this to me so I can pay them back for what they did."

"I can do that, we can't have people coming into my city and making a mess without me knowing about it."

"Thanks Frankie, I owe you one for this."

Frankie waved him off and started to eat again.

Buck and Rachael watched as Ice Man left the building and drove off. Buck looked at Rachael, "Are you ready to go?"

"Let's find out who Ice Man was talking to first. Then we can go."

Waiting another 30 minutes Frankie and his two bodyguards walked out of the restaurant to their car. Buck started the truck up and proceeded to follow Frankie. When they reached the Frontier Hotel, Frankie got out of the car and went inside the hotel with two more bodyguards in tow. Buck dropped Rachael off at the entrance as well so she could follow Frankie. Frankie walked past the front desk and went directly to the elevators, and with Rachael watching as the elevator went up to the penthouse floor. Rachael came back outside where Buck was waiting, and after she got back into the truck they drove off.

"Did you see where he went?" Buck asked.

"The penthouse floor, this should be easy to find out who it is and what he's planning on doing," Rachael replied.

"I can hardly wait to find out."

Chapter VII

When Buck and Rachael got back to Gared and Tina's place they were feeling pretty tired, so much so, all they wanted to do was sleep. Tina had made dinner for the kids and Gared as well, and everybody was at the table eating when Buck and Rachael came into the kitchen. Without hesitating, Tina grabbed a couple of plates of food and set it down on the table in front of them to eat. Buck hadn't given any thought about eating earlier and when he sat down to eat he realized he was really hungry for the first time today. Rachael didn't waste any time eating either and it made Tina happy when both Buck and Rachael asked for seconds.

When Buck finished eating he called Evans and as he was waiting for Evans to pick up the phone Rachael came in and sat down next to him. Evans answered the phone, "Hello, what have you found?"

"We found Ice Man's place of operation and if you were to go there right now you would find a mess of drugs in one of the rooms that's locked,"

Buck replied.

"We'll look into getting a warrant to look inside his place," Evans replied.

"Oh, one other thing we need to know about a guy that lives in the penthouse of the Frontier Hotel. He had two goons with him when he got out of the car at the lobby of the hotel."

"I'll look into that as well. How about dinner tonight?"

"Thanks, but we just ate. How about tomorrow night? We'll save ourselves and go from there."

"Fair enough, how about sevenish?"

"That would be fine, till then, good night."

"Good night, oh by the way Mako is at the Sahara Hospital room 204, just so you know," Evans said.

"Thanks for the update, we'll see you two tomorrow night," Buck replied.

Buck hung up the phone and told Rachael, "Mako is in the Sahara Hospital recovering in room 204. Do you feel up to visiting him tonight?"

"Do you think he'll remember us? You know we only met him once, he might have forgotten all about us," Rachael said as she smiled.

Buck looked at her, and laughing said, "We may need to refresh his memory a little, what do you think?"

"Could be, we need to at least try. I really don't want him to forget us, seeing as how we've become such close friends."

Buck and Rachael talked to Miguel after the phone call, "Miguel, we found Ice Man's place and searched it for the girls, they were not there and neither was the van."

"What happened?" Miguel asked.

"Not much we left him a message that we were in the area and are still looking for him and the girls," Rachael replied.

Miguel was getting upset, "What happens if he kills both of the girls?"

"He won't, simply because it is his only bargaining chip to get you and Tim. They're both alive we just need to find out where they are and bring them home safe and sound," Buck answered.

"The sooner, the better for all involved," Rachael added.

Buck grabbed Miguel by the shoulders, "We won't let anything happen to any of you kids, you got to believe me when I say this."

Miguel looked him in the eyes and knew that look of determination and resolve and knew that he meant it. "I believe you," Miguel said.

Rachael gave Miguel a hug, "I know this is

hard, but we are making headway. We are going to find the girls and bring them home."

Marissa and Jennifer were sitting in the room all by themselves, scared and at the same time bored. Marissa wondered where Miguel was and when they were coming to get them. Jennifer was crying so Marissa crawled over to where she heard the crying, and touched her hand to let her know she wasn't alone. The girls were trying to be brave, but under the circumstances it was hard thing to do. Feeling all alone and not knowing where they were or if anybody else was looking for them, just added to their being scared.

Marissa heard footsteps coming down the hallway from outside the room, the door opened, and she could tell that they were placing something by them. Marissa froze, not knowing what to do. Pretty soon her head cover was taken off, and the flash of light hurt her eyes. She squinted, taking a minute to let her eyes to adjust to seeing normally again.

"You need to go to the bathroom?" the man said.

Marissa nodded yes, afraid to say anything. The man picked her up from the floor and took her into the bathroom. He loosened the rope around her wrists and said, "Don't try anything funny or your friend gets it."

Marissa nodded yes, and closed the door behind her. Coming out a couple minutes later he took her back to the room and told her to eat. He then took Jennifer to the bathroom as well and in a couple of minutes they were together eating the food the man had brought them.

Marissa looked at Jennifer, "How are you doing?"

Jennifer still eating said, "Better now that we got some food to eat."

Marissa looked at her, "I think they moved us so that whoever is looking for us can't find us."

Jennifer looked up, stopped eating and started crying again, "There never going to find us, are they?"

"I think it's the other way around someone is looking for us and there moving us because the people that are looking for us are getting closer."

"I really hope so, I'm scared and I don't want to die."

"I'm scared to, and I don't want to die either. So all we can do is keep hoping that whoever is looking for us will find us soon."

By now, the man reappeared in the room and took the tray of food and tied them up again, this time leaving the hoods off and their mouths untapped. Marissa and Jennifer huddled together for warmth and security, all the while praying that they would be found before it was too late.

Buck and Rachael drove to the Sahara Hospital and walked the halls till they found room 204. Seeing no one outside guarding the room and checking that there was no else inside the room, they walked in and stood there a moment. Mako who was asleep, opened his eyes and just about screamed. Buck quickly covered his mouth and using his finger to cover his lips whispered, "shush," to Mako.

Rachael watched the door and nodded to Buck. He quietly whispered in Mako's ear, "You know I'm surprised you made it back to Vegas, now I owe my wife five dollars because I bet that you wouldn't make it back."

Mako's eyes were as wide as saucers by now and he was ready to run and hide. For that reason, Buck had him pinned to the bed so he couldn't move. Rachael came over, "You know, Mako you lied to us."

Mako was shaking his head no, with a look of fear in his eyes remembering what had happened the last time he lied.

"Yes, you did. You told us that the girls would be there at Ice Man's place and you know what, they weren't there. That means you lied to us, and that's why we're back."

Mako rolled his eyes and whimpered not knowing what to do.

Rachael looked at him again, "My partner is going to remove his hand from your mouth and you're going to tell us where the girls are now. Now, before he removes his hand, I'm going to warn you if you scream or try to get away we will kill you for sure and there's nothing you can do to stop it. The nurses will be too late to help, do you understand?"

Mako nodded, yes, and waited for Buck to remove his hand from off his mouth. "I don't know where he took the girls, all I know is that he had them with him to trade for the pictures," Mako said.

"Does Ice Man have friends in Vegas?" Buck asked.

Mako though for a moment, "He has the backing of the syndicate here in town; they do all his dirty work when he wants to keep his hands clean."

"Do his friends live in the Frontier Hotel?" Rachael asked.

"Yes, they do, it's the headquarters for the syndicate's city-wide operations."

Buck asked one more question, "Do you know if Ice Man has another place to live around here?"

Mako looked at them with fear in his eyes. "Yes, but I don't know where it is. All I know for sure it's not in the valley."

With that, Buck and Rachael were ready to leave the hospital room. As they were leaving, Rachael looked at Mako and said, "If you're lying and we catch you at it, we'll be coming back to visit again and next time you will not be leaving the hospital through the front door, do you understand?"

Mako looked at them and nodded his head yes and closed his eyes, hoping they would be gone when he opened them again. When he opened his eyes again they were gone and he breathed a sigh of relief, ringing the nurse for some more pain killers for his leg.

Buck and Rachael sat in the truck trying to decide what to do next. They now knew that the syndicate was involved in getting them and that was going to make things a little harder finding the girls and Ice Man.

"Who do we go after first, the syndicate or Ice Man?" Rachael asked.

Buck thought on this for a moment, "Let's get them together again and take them both at the same time."

"What about the goons from the syndicate?"

"With the help of Metro and the FBI, we should be able to stop them."

"What about the mole?"

"We go after him first."

"The question is, how do we find him."

"With the help of Evans and Linda, we should be able to trap him. The only thing different is that we can't go back to Gared and Tina's house for a while after tonight."

Buck and Rachael went back to the house looking for Gared, Tina and Miguel. After finding them, Buck had them all come into the den.

"We need to let you know what we're doing. Rachael and I are going under cover for a while and won't be coming around much in the near future."

"What's up?" Gared asked.

"We found the place where Ice Man is running his business out of and we kind of messed it up for him. Now he wants us out of the picture and so to protect you guys and Tim we're going under the radar. This way, you won't be worried about us not being around for a while."

"Is there anything we can do to help?" Tina asked.

"You've done more than we could've hoped

for. Feeding us and taking care of the kids. It has been a real pleasure having you guys here for us. We couldn't have done this without you," Rachael replied.

"It's better we leave here and do this our way than have any of you good people get hurt. We would never forgive ourselves if that happened," Buck said.

"Us, either. We'll take care of the boys." Gared and Tina said, laughing.

"Miguel, we will find the girls so don't worry yourself sick over it," Rachael said.

After their conversation, Buck and Rachael stepped out into the darkness and got into their truck and drove away. Buck and Rachael didn't have a clue of where to go first, all they knew was that their world was about to get busy and crowded. Buck and Rachael found a dive motel for a place to lay low that didn't ask any questions and only took cash for a deposit for the room they rented. That being done, and having a base to operate from, they went to bed and lay there in the darkness trying to sleep. Rachael took Bucks hand, "I think with a little work we could make this place kind of nice to live in."

Buck chuckled, "Kind of reminds me of when we were dating."

"Now that you mention it, I knew there was something familiar about it. It's just like your place when we met the first time when I came over."

"I think this may have been cleaner than my bachelor pad."

Buck rolled over and put his arms around her, "Did you ever think we would be having this much fun in Las Vegas?"

"I had no idea we could do all of this and not lose a dime at the slots and this hotel is all the rave back in Phoenix. I'm sure glad we were able to get the penthouse for so little and at the peak season as well."

"Is this a Kodak moment?"

"I think so?"

The next morning, Buck and Rachael went down into the street and walked to the Denny's on the corner and had breakfast. Looking out the window of the booth they were sitting at, they watched one person pushing their belongings in a grocery cart pass the window. Buck looked back at Rachael, "Who do we follow first the rookie or the old timer?"

"The old timer first, there was something strange about him I didn't like when we met him the first time."

They drove their truck to the federal building

and sat outside watching for either of the two resident field agents to show up for work. Warren was the first show and after ten minutes, Jenkins showed up, as well. They waited till both were inside the building before walking over to their vehicles to look inside them. Buck took Jenkins car and Rachael took Warren's vehicle. Rachael went through the jockey box hoping to find something incriminating but all she found was the typical insurance and ownership records for the car. Searching the back seat and under the front seats she found some paperwork dealing with money transactions at the bank he used. The paperwork showed deposits of money in the amounts of $500 dollars each to his bank account. Rachael kept these receipts to show Buck.

Buck went through Jenkins car, after getting through the food wrappers and drinking cups he found nothing other than the typical bachelor stuff in the car. Checking the jockey box, as well, Buck found nothing incriminating for Jenkins. After getting back to the truck, he found that Rachael was already there waiting for him.

Buck looked at her, "Next time you get the bachelor and I'll get the old timer."

"Look what I found," said Racheal holding up the deposit slips.

"How many of them are there?"

"I found three of them, all totaling 1500 dollars."

"Maybe he's got a rich aunt who likes him."

"We need to go to his bank and look at his records."

"How do we do that without a warrant?" asked Buck.

"Don't you know I've got friends in the right places that can help us?"

Buck and Racheal thought it wise to check in with Evans and Linda at this time. So, they casually walked into the FBI office and stopped into where Evans and Linda were going through the records. The place looked a lot better than it did when they found Sherron on the floor the other day. Evans and Linda were surprised to see them in the office. Evans came out from the interior office and shook Buck's hand, "To what do we owe this visit from such avid travelers from Arizona?"

Linda looked at him, "Oh for heaven's sake Evans, stop with the tourist stuff."

Evans looks at her smiling, "Yes dear."

Buck laughed. "How long you guys been married? It took Rachael three years to get me to learn that."

Evans looked at him smiling, "I guess I'm

smarter than you, huh?"

Buck laughed. "Ouch that almost hurts."

Linda, looking at both of them, laughed. "Don't be fooled if I didn't remind once a day I was in charge he'd be lost."

"That really hurts now, oh the pain, the agony, oh yeah, marriage," Evans replied feigning the hurt.

Rachael looked at them laughing, "Where did we find such poor examples of slaves, err, I mean men?"

"Well, you know we don't have to stand here and take this abuse, or do we?" Buck said, looking shocked.

"We do," Evans replied.

"Rats, I was afraid you were going to say that."

With all the joking done the ladies went into the inner office following the Buck and Evans. Once seated and the door closed Evans said, "So what brings you here so early in the morning?"

Buck responded to the question by detailing what they had learned about the syndicate being based in the Frontier Hotel on the Strip and about talking to Mako once again.

"Did he have any more to say about Ice Man or his whereabouts?" Evans asked.

"Supposedly, Ice Man has another place that

he calls home, not in the valley, but close by. Can you look into it for us? I have a feeling that is where the girls are at right now," Buck said.

"Can do," Evans said.

"What about Warren and Jenkins? Where are they? We just watched them come in the building," asked Rachael.

"Nothing yet on either one of them so far. We have a satellite office down the hall and that's where we have them for right now, seeing as how this office isn't big enough for four people."

"I meant to ask about Sherron, how is she doing?" asked Rachael.

"She's still in the hospital, but she will fully recover," replied Linda

"That's good news," said Rachael.

Rachael then laid out the three bank deposit receipts from Warren's car that she had found. Linda looked at them, then passed them onto Evans. Both looked grim with the new information laid out before them.

"Our first lead," Linda nodded in agreement with Evan's statement. "We will look into this as well," Evans said.

"We checked both cars and this is all we found so far. I think we should do like we did in Miami. Count on everything being bugged and we meet at other places to talk," Buck said.

Evans and Linda both agreed with Buck on this one.

"Let me call Warren and Jenkins in to see if they have picked up anything from the street." After calling them Evans hung up the phone with a look of concern on his face.

"According to Jenkins, the word on the street is, the syndicate has put a hit out on two people that messed with one of their clients. I assume you guys are it. Please be extra cautious out there and watch your six."

Buck and Rachael looked surprised and yet not surprised by this new bit of information. "Looks like we stepped on the right toes here in town. We'll be careful out there," said Buck.

As Buck and Rachael said their goodbyes to Evans and Linda they walked out to the truck and sat there waiting for the truck to get warmed up.

"This changes everything, we need to cancel the hit first, and then go after Ice Man," Buck said.

"I agree, we'll let Evans and Linda deal with the leak in their office," said Rachael.

As they drove out of the parking lot, they turned right onto the street in front of the Federal Building and headed up the street stopping at the red light. Waiting for the signal to turn green, Buck noticed a motorcycle in his rearview mirror coming up from on his side of the truck. Seeing as how the bike wasn't going to stop soon, Buck floored the gas pedal and jumped out into the intersection, almost hitting a car, but clearing the intersection and going onto the other side driving as fast as he could. Rachael, by now, was aware that they were being chased by the motorcyclist, grabbed her gun, and turned herself to face the motorcyclist, prepared to fire. The motorcyclist narrowly avoided another car as he went through the same intersection following Buck and Rachael. As the motorcyclist got closer to the truck, Buck turned his steering wheel in the direction of the bike, broad-siding the bike and rider with his truck, causing the motorcycle to lay out on the pavement with the rider pinned beneath the bike. Once the bike stopped moving, Buck and Racheal were out of the truck with their guns pulled, pointing at the rider. The rider, unable to pull his own gun, lay there and waited for the two of them to get there.

As he lay there, Rachael kept a gun on him while Buck took his helmet off of him. It was an older man who was riding the bike and he knew he was done for. Rachael called 911 for Metro PD to come and get the rider. The Metro officers showed up in record time and after taking Buck and Rachael's statements they were free to leave. After running the name of the motorcyclist, Metro found that he was wanted on a warrant in connection to a murder for hire in Los Angeles, California. Buck looked at the man as he was being put in the back of the squad car. Buck shook his head as he walked back to the truck where Rachael was sitting. He got in the driver's side of the truck and kept shaking his head in bewilderment.

Rachael reached out and touched him, "You alright?"

"No, I'm not, this is the closest I've ever been to losing you and I don't like the feeling," Buck replied.

Rachael sat for a moment, "It's going to take a lot more for you to lose me especially with a hitman on a motorcycle. We need to go after the man that ordered the hit and get him to change his mind about it."

Buck looked at her and realized she was angry about what had almost happened.

"You know I was thinking about you the same way. Now let's go get this son of a gun and teach him a lesson about our facts of life," Rachael said.

With that, Buck put the truck into gear and

drove to the Frontier Hotel. After arriving in the parking lot, Buck and Rachael walked to the main lobby and made their way to the elevators. Getting on the elevators and going to highest floor they got off and made their way to the fire escape and went upstairs and from there onto the roof. Checking out the roof, they found a ladder that went down to the penthouse. Lying flat on his belly, Buck looked over the edge of the roof and looked inside the penthouse sliding glass windows. Seeing nobody around, Buck crawled back to where Rachael was waiting, "The coast is clear if we want to go in and wait."

Rachael nodded her head in agreement, "What is the best way to get in without being seen?"

Buck thought about this for a minute, "How about we go through the elevator top and pry the doors to the elevator open and go through that way."

Rachael thought about it for a second and smiling, "Will it mess up my hair, you know I just had it done the other day?"

Buck looked at her, "You did?"

Rachael smacked him for that, "Let's go, were burning daylight, smarty."

Buck and Rachael made their way back down into the stairway and went to the elevator and pressed the button. In two minutes the elevator doors opened, and going in, Buck locked the elevator in place. He then crawled up into the overhead area of the elevator, standing on top of the elevator he found a ladder inside the elevator shaft and started to climb up the ladder to the penthouse floor.

Rachael, watching all of this, closed the cover to the elevator behind her and crawled out onto the top of the elevator as well; making her way to the ladder she crawled up behind Buck and waited. Buck pulled out his knife and wedged it between the doors of the penthouse suite, opening the doors. The doors opened a crack, enabling Buck to peer through, and seeing that no one was there, he forced the doors open wider and told Rachael, "Climb over me and I'll follow you."

With his gun out, he held the doors open for Rachael as she climbed through, into the penthouse. After getting on the main floor, Rachael held the doors open for Buck with her gun out, watching for anyone that might be there. Once Buck and Rachael were inside the penthouse, they did a quick sweep of the rooms to make sure there were no surprises or guns hanging around. At this point it was a matter of time for Frankie to show up and be met by Buck and Rachael. After Buck and Rachael finished going through the penthouse, they took all of the guns they found and dumped them in the elevator shaft on top of the elevator.

Buck looked at Rachael, "Are you hungry?"

"Yes, I wonder what a mobster eats. I'm thinking it should be pretty good with all of the money he has to spend," Rachael replied.

Buck looked at her and said, "Let's go find out."

They walked into the kitchen and started rummaging through the cupboards and refrigerator. After about five minutes of looking they came up with some caviar and cheese with some crackers to eat.

"Do you think he'll mind us helping ourselves to this food? I know how some people are very particular about others going through their refrigerator without their permission first," Rachael asked.

"If he has any complaints he can tell us about it himself."

Rachael nodded. "Works for me."

After lunch Rachael went back into the kitchen and found some Champagne in the refrigerator and brought it out, "Look what I found," showing it to Buck, "This stuff can kill you, I'd better pour it down the drain for him. I know he'll thank us for it later."

By now it, was close to 5:00 pm and the sun was starting go behind the mountains in the west desert.

At about 6:00 pm, the elevator was running again and Buck and Rachael knew that eventually Frankie would be coming up to his penthouse. At 6:30 pm the penthouse doors opened and Frankie came walking in. Heading to the bathroom to relieve himself, he closed the door and sat down. Buck and Rachael waited for him outside the bathroom door. After he flushed the toilet he walked out the door and that's when Buck hit him in the back of the head. Frankie fell to the floor and landed on his hands and knees briefly stunned. Rachael told him not to move as Buck frisked him. Finding Frankie's gun, Buck threw it in the toilet and then grabbing him by the collar of his shirt, dragged him to the couch. Frankie, realizing he wasn't alone, started to scream and Buck hit him in the face with his gun. Frankie fell back onto the couch holding his face and head as blood trickled from his nose.

Buck sat down in the chair opposite Frankie, "I think we need to introduce ourselves to you. We are the people you put a contract out on yesterday and we're here to tell you to call it off now or it's going to get real hard for you to pay it."

"Especially, if your dead," said Rachael.

Frankie looked confused at first and then his head started to clear a little. The first thing Frankie asked was, "How did you get in here?"

"We took the elevator up," Buck replied.

Frankie started to get mad and began threatening Buck and Rachael on how he was going to kill both of them. Rachael looked at Buck and Buck nodded at Rachael, with that, she shot him in the knee cap. Frankie screamed in pain at being shot and started to hold his knee because of the excruciating pain as it was bleeding on the floor. Buck looked at Frankie Diamond, "Call off the hit or the next shot won't be your knee, in fact it could be a little higher if you know what I mean."

"You have a phone, don't you? How about you call that special someone that will cancel the hit?" Rachael asked.

Frankie, looking at Rachael and Buck, said, "Yes," as he groaned in pain.

"That's a good boy, now make the call," Buck said

Frankie, using his cell phone, dialed the number and after hearing it ring twice a voice on the other end said, "Yeah, boss?"

At this time, Buck put his semi-auto next to Frankie's head and cocked the trigger back on his gun. Frankie, heard the gun being cocked, "Call off the hit on the two people."

The voice on the other end said, "But boss, we just set it up yesterday."

Frankie, yelled at the guy on the other end of the phone, "I changed my mind, are you questioning me?"

The voice on the phone said, "No sir."

"Then do it!" Frankie said as he hung up the phone.

"See, that wasn't hard at all, was it Frankie," Buck said.

Frankie looked at Buck, "I'm going to kill you myself, do you hear me?"

Buck fired his gun hitting Frankie in the other knee blowing his kneecap out. Frankie screaming again in pain, now holding both knees this time, looked up at Buck.

"I really do wish you would try, right now in fact," Buck said smiling.

By now the elevator was operating again, and reaching the penthouse, the door opened with two of Frankie's men coming out of the elevator carrying guns. Rachael shot them both in quick succession, hitting each of them in the forehead, both of the men went down bleeding in the entrance to the penthouse.

Buck slapped Frankie in the face, "Do you want to try it?"

Frankie, seeing his men go down, realized he had met his match, looked down at his knees, "No, I don't think so."

Rachael looked at him, "If we even think someone is following us, we will come back and throw you off the top of the hotel. DO YOU UNDERSTAND Frankie?"

Frankie shook his head, yes. This time, Buck hit him again saying, "The lady asked you a question. Do you understand?"

"Yes, I understand!" Frankie screamed.

As Buck and Rachael were leaving the penthouse, Rachael looked at Frankie, "Oh, by the way, we had some lunch up here while waiting for you. You're running low on the caviar and cheese, and you really shouldn't be drinking the champagne, it's not good for you. We found some in the refrigerator and poured it down the drain, no need to thank me for it; I was just thinking of your health."

Buck looked back at Frankie while they were in the elevator, "You tell Ice Man we're coming for him and if anything has happened to the girls he won't live to see another day." Looking at Frankie, Buck continued, "Man, housekeeping is going to be upset with the mess here in the foyer. Remember, anytime and anyplace, Frankie."

Buck and Rachael took the elevator down to the lobby and walked out into the sunset with Buck saying, "It's almost time for dinner with Evans and Linda, shall we call them and let them know we're ready to go?"

"Yes, let's do, I'm famished! You think Frankie would have had more food in his refrigerator," Rachael replied.

As they drove off, Buck and Rachael could hear the sirens of the ambulance and police cars as they made their way to the Frontier Hotel lobby.

Chapter VIII

The ambulance had just left the Frontier Hotel with Frankie laying on the gurney completely passed out from the drugs. Ice Man was visibly shaken when he saw the damage done to Frankie's legs. He knew Frankie was going to live but being confined to a wheel chair wasn't his idea of living any kind of life. It was what Frankie said to Ice Man that hit close to home for him. It was the threat the man said when he stated that he was coming after Ice Man, that shook him up the most.

As he was helping with the cleanup of Frankie's bodyguards, before the ambulance came up to the penthouse, Ice Man had seen with his own eyes, the damage done to Frankie. This was the first time Ice Man started to melt. Anybody crazy enough to go after Frankie in his own place was somebody not to be messed with. And seeing how the contract hit was called off, Ice Man, after regaining his composure, decided to go after the two people who had done this to Frankie. No matter the cost of life, it was now about Ice Man against these two people. It was a matter of principle, a matter of who was in control. Ice Man was not going to blink first in this game of chicken.

Ice Man, after leaving the penthouse, walking through the casino pulled out his cell phone and made a call to his old stomping ground buddies in Fresno.

Listening to the phone ring, the line went active, and a voice on the other end answered, "This had better be important."

Ice Man replied, "Oh, it is, very important. I need to speak with Dominic."

Dominic answered the phone, "What ya need?"

"Send Tommy out here now."

"No problem," and hung up the phone.

Ice Man knew that this was his only way of staying out of jail for the drug shipment. He had the photos and the girls for leverage, now he needed to get rid of the two people that had taken Frankie out, and the only one that could do this now was Tommy.

The next day it was in all the local newspapers about how a gangland hit occurred in the Frontier Hotel, leaving two men dead and one injured. The police had no leads to follow-up on simply because the survivor refused to talk.

Even though Metro police department really wasn't concerned about who did it knowing that the survivor was part of the syndicate. After Ice Man had read the article about the hit on his friend, Frankie, he realized things had escalated beyond his capabilities. Tommy was the answer for all of his problems, yet in the back of his mind his doubts were still forming and he wondered to himself if Tommy would even be able to do what was necessary to stop these two people. He knew that his only insurance was the two girls and he knew, from what Frankie had said, that harming the girls in any way would cost him dearly. Ice man wasn't afraid, or at least he didn't think he was, but to be safe the girls would remain unharmed for a little while longer.

Buck and Rachael both knew that the gauntlet had been thrown down in front of Ice Man. Ice Man would have to pick it up and he would have to answer the challenge. Buck also knew that time was running out for the girls and they had to act fast. By telling Ice Man they were coming after him, Buck was hoping to buy some more time for the girls. Rachael understood why and what Buck's reasons were as to what he did to Frankie. People like Frankie and Ice Man, you don't reason with. The only thing they understand is that whoever is in charge has to be more dangerous than them and you did this by being meaner than they were. The minions respected power through intimidation and pain. That is, being more willing to hurt the opponent, just as much, if not more, than they would. Any sign of compassion or mercy was a sign of weakness to be capitalized on. Ice Man understood this psychology of control and power and how to use it, and the minions that followed respected the ones who would be willing to inflict more pain than their opponents would. Hence, Ice Man had met his match on the playing field of Las Vegas with Buck and Rachael. Ice Man's answer to the threat on his control and power was Tommy.

Tommy was an animal who walked on two feet and looked human. That was all that was human about Tommy. Tommy was a killing machine that had survived by being tougher than his opponents. He had no soul or conscience to get in his way of doing his kind of business. Tommy knew only one thing and that was to kill whoever got in his way. He was the illegitimate offspring of a mother who was addicted to meth that pulled tricks to get the drugs she craved in order to live. She had died from an overdose and left six-year-old Tommy to the foster care of the state. In and out of foster homes for the next twelve years to be set free from the system on his eighteenth birthday to roam the streets of Fresno California. Because of his size and strength, he had learned he had a talent as an enforcer which graduated to killing people. If there was a creature that would characterize him it would have to be a great white shark with its black soulless eyes.

Tommy rode the bus up to Las Vegas and was picked up by one of Ice Man's men at the bus depot. He rode in the car back to Ice Man's place, not saying a word, just waiting to meet Ice Man. When Ice Man's men delivered Tommy to the warehouse he was met by Ice Man and only then did Tommy smile, recognizing his old boss from California. Tommy had formed an attachment to Ice Man something of the sorts of a male figure in Tommy's life. Ice Man had taken Tommy under his proverbial wing to nurture him. He treated Tommy well and always gave him gifts after he completed the job he was sent to carry out. Ice Man had learned that Tommy was not all there, he figured it out when it came to having him do things for him. For Tommy, Ice Man was his best and only friend and always treated him good, never got upset with him and always had something for him. Sometimes it was money or gifts, like watches and clothes and other stuff. The one bond that Tommy had with the real world was with Ice Man, other than Ice Man the world for Tommy was empty. There was no love, no mercy, and no compassion, no anything that normal people sometimes take for granted.

Ice man grabbed Tommy and hugged him, "Hey Tommy how are you doing? Glad to see you again."

Tommy responded to Ice Man by smiling and hugging him back, "Tommy miss you, and why have you been gone from Tommy for so long?"

"Well, I have been kind of busy and couldn't get away to come and visit Tommy like I wanted to."

Tommy smiled. "Aw that's okay, Tommy here now."

"Yes, you are, and I need you to do me a favor, can you do that for Ice Man?"

"Oh boy just like old times, huh, Ice Man? What do you want Tommy to do?"

"Yes, it is. Now Tommy, I need you to listen to me. There are some bad people following me and they want to hurt me. Do you understand?"

Tommy eyes grew narrow and he had a mean look on his face saying, "Where are these bad people? Tommy will find them and hurt them for Ice Man. Nobody hurt my friend Ice Man"

"That's good Tommy, really good. I will show you where these bad people are soon, just wait until I find them."

"Tommy wait till Ice Man find them, then Tommy will hurt bad people for Ice Man."

"Tommy, I need you to go sit over there in the chair, and wait till I'm ready to leave."

Tommy went and sat down next to the TV and started quietly watching the cartoon channel.

Buck and Rachael had just finished dinner with Evans and Linda, and after asking for Evans to do a background check on Ice Man for finances, they were on their way back to the dive motel they were staying in. Upon arriving at the motel, Buck checked inside their room by pushing the door open and waiting before going inside. Once Buck was sure that the room was clear, they went in and sat down on the bed and the only chair in the room.

"Now that we got the hit cancelled, how do we find the girls?" Buck said.

"We wait for Evans to get us the information about the house that Ice Man owns. Hopefully, he will find it in the finances of Ice Man," Rachael replied.

"Did we ever check the green van that was in the pictures that Tim took?"

"No, we didn't. Do you have the other set of pictures handy?"

"They're right here in the suitcase."

Buck pulled them out and handed them to Rachael; she scanned them, "I can barely make out the license plate number on the van. How about we go to Metro and ask them to run the plates for us, including the type of van and anything else we can think of."

Buck and Rachael drove to the local police station and asked the desk sergeant if he would run the plates for them. After showing their badges, the desk sergeant directed them to the auto theft division down the hall. In five minutes, the van came back with the plates being registered to a Mr. Bronson with an address of 1221 Aspen Way. Not knowing where this was Buck asked, "Do you know where this address is?"

The sergeant in auto theft, using his computer, looked up the address and found it. Taking a minute to get his bearings the sergeant said, "It's up in the Mt. Charleston area."

After printing a map for them, the sergeant gave Buck and Rachael directions on how to get to Mt. Charleston. They in turn thanked him and left the police station.

Buck and Rachael went to their truck, got in

and left the parking lot of the police station. Driving interstate 15 and taking the turn off for Beatty, they started heading north on state route 95, then taking the Mt. Charleston turnoff they headed into the mountains. The drive up to Mt. Charleston was quiet and cool as they climbed in elevation as they drove to get to the mountain. In the rear-view mirror, you could see Las Vegas lit up like a big carnival at night. The glow of the lights could be seen for miles in any direction. From a distance, it was a glow that took up the whole horizon, and as you got closer to the city, the different hotels would give off their own individual lights, identifying to the driver where the hotel was on the Strip.

Upon reaching the Mt. Charleston lodge, Buck and Rachael noticed that the pine trees that were common at this altitude were as tall as 100 feet or more, and they were blocking the lights of Las Vegas. From here the stars were clear and bright and went on forever. Buck and Rachael began looking for the address on Aspen Way. As they made their way through the streets, Buck stopped the truck, "Hey, isn't that a green van up there?"

Rachael, looking at the picture of the van and checking the license plate number confirmed, "Yes that's the one in the picture."

Pulling over to the side of the road Buck and Rachael got out of the truck and gently closed the doors so as not to attract any attention. Buck, staying in the shadows walked up to the house and looking through the windows, could see two men inside. He could tell they were carrying guns but that was all he could see from his vantage point. He moved from window to window around the house, with the shades pulled down, he couldn't see much in the house. One room had a light on inside but the blinds and drapes were closed. He went back to the window and watched the two men sitting in the front room. One of them got up and made his way to the kitchen, bringing out a tray of food and headed back to one of the bedrooms. When he came back without the tray, Buck realized that there was someone else in the house. Making his way back to the truck he gave the thumbs up signal to Rachael. After getting back to the truck he said, "There's someone else in the house besides the two men.

Looking relieved that they had found the girls she said, "I have an Idea as how to get in the house and get the girls out."

"It's your show."

"I need you to go back to the house and wait by the kitchen door. Open it and wait till I knock on the front door. When I've got their attention, you draw down on them and I'll cover them as well, no muss, no fuss, what do you think?"

"What happens if the door is locked?"

"I will unlock it for you before I go to the front door."

"I like it, let's do it, give me five minutes to get to the back door, okay?"

Rachael nodded her head and left the truck, checking her watch, "See you on the other side."

Buck took off into the darkness. After five minutes, Rachael went to the house and knocked on the door. One of the men got up and came over and opened the door, "What do you want?"

"My car just quit on me and I need a tow truck to come move it for me. My cell phone died and I have no way to call. Can I use your phone and make the call for the tow truck?"

The other man asked, "What's going on?"

"I need to use your phone, my car just died and my cellphone is dead."

"Harry, let her use your cell phone," The second man said.

By now, Buck was inside and was standing in the kitchen watching Rachael do her part. Buck yelled, "Drop your guns now and raise your hands in the air!" Rachael pulled her gun and kept them covered while Buck collected their weapons. Both men were then told to lay on the ground face first and hands behind their backs. Rachael zip tied their legs and hands making sure they couldn't move. Buck stayed there to watch them as Rachael went through each room looking for the girls and after a couple of minutes found them; she walked into the room and cut their ropes off their hands. The girls started to cry, knowing that they were safe now and were going home. She wrapped them in the blankets that were on the floor and took them out to where the truck was parked.

After that, Rachael came back in the house, "The girls are safe, now we need to have a talk with you gentlemen. Where can we find Ice Man?"

The two men had no idea how to locate him except at the warehouse. Buck then asked, "Do you have Ice Man's phone number in one of your cell phones?"

Harry started to say something when his partner told him, "Shut up, don't say nothing at all, you hear me."

At this point, Rachael shot Harry's partner in the back of the leg causing him to scream. Harry, realizing what had happened, yelled, "It's on the table in the front room!"

Buck went and got the cell phone, found the

number, wrote it down and as they were leaving Buck said, "Harry, you need to take your friend to the doctor or he could bleed out on the floor next to you and thanks for the number."

"I'm not worried about my partner, but I'd be worried about you and your partner," Harry said.

Buck stopped dead in his tracks and turned around, "What does that mean?"

Harry replied, laughing, "You'll see soon enough, you may need the hospital more than my partner does."

Buck and Rachael were talking about what Harry had said on the way back to the truck. Wondering what he meant Rachael said, "We need to find Ice Man and follow him to find out what he has up his sleeve for us."

"I agree, maybe we can case his place to see what pops up. For right now we need to get these girls back to Tina and Gared's place."

Buck and Rachael got into the truck and headed back to Vegas to take the girls home. The girls were still crying when they pulled up to the front of the house. Buck and Rachael walked them to the door. Knocking on the door, Tina and Miguel answered the door and let them in. Rachael went into the house while Buck stood by the door watching. The girls went to their respective boyfriends and hugged them, still crying yet glad to be home. Miguel looked at Buck and mouthed the words, "Thank you dad."

"You're welcome son," Buck said.

Tim, now able to move around a little more, took Jennifer and holding her and looking at Rachael said, "How can I thank you for this?"

"You don't need to, we were glad to be able to find the girls and bring them back safely. We will need to talk to them when they get settled in again, probably in a couple of days."

"Should be no problem once they get a good night's sleep and some good food in them," Tina said.

"I know about your good cooking, for sure that should fix them up," Rachael said.

Rachael and Buck left the house and drove back to their dive hotel room. After getting ready for bed, Buck and Rachael lay there thinking about all that had happened since they got the phone call from Miguel which had brought them to Las Vegas. They were thinking about the pictures, dealing with Mako, the kidnapping of the girls, Frankie, and the Ice Man. After considering the steps they took to close each one of these issues, Rachael said, "So far we have been very lucky getting done what we have accomplished. The two things that stand out now are the leak and Ice Man."

"Our main concern now lies with finding the informant that almost got us killed. Worst of all he's still out there running loose, and the question is how much does he know about us?" Buck said.

By now Buck, could barely keep his eyes open and soon was fast asleep. Rachael was still talking to him when Buck fell asleep. Upon not getting any reply to her questions, Rachael looked down at Buck and realizing he was fast asleep, kissed him on the forehead and lay down next to him and whispered, "I love you, I guess we've done enough for today," and fell asleep as well.

Chapter IX

The next morning found Buck and Rachael still in bed, when the cell phone started ringing. Buck answered the phone quickly so as not to wake up Rachael, "Hello."

The voice on the other end of the phone identified herself as Linda, "Something terrible has happened to Evans, can you two get over to the Sahara Hospital, ASAP?"

"What happened to Evans?

"He's been shot in the abdomen and he's here in the emergency room."

"Is he going to make it?"

By now, Linda was crying over the phone and was barely coherent, "I don't know, it's too soon to tell."

Buck, waking up Rachael said, "Give us a couple of minutes and we'll be right over."

Buck told Rachael about Evans having been shot and being in the emergency room as they quickly dressed and made their way to the hospital. Upon arriving at the hospital, they found the information desk and asked where they could find the emergency room then proceeded to find their way there. Seeing Linda pacing the floor, Rachael reached her first. Holding her, she let Linda cry.

After a couple of minutes Buck asked, "What happened to Evans, how did he get shot?"

All Linda could do for the moment was cry, and let her emotions run for the time being. After a couple of more minutes Linda composed herself, looking at both of them, "We were checking the background on Warren and Jenkins and as usual we went to the bank where the money had been deposited as listed on the receipts you gave us. When we went in we saw Warren in there and he took off out the back of the bank. Evans followed him out of the bank and Warren pulled his gun and shot Evans. After being hit, Evans returned fire, hitting Warren in the shoulder before he went down."

"How is he?" Rachael asked.

"He's in the operating room being worked on right now."

"Did the doctors say anything about his condition?"

"No, they just took him into the operating room and left me here."

Buck went over to the emergency room desk and asked the lady sitting there if there was anything new on the status of Evans. The receptionist, picked up the phone and called back to the ICU section. The nurse working at the station said, "He's still in the operating room and there is nothing new to report at this time."

Buck came back and shaking his head, "Nothing yet."

Holding both Rachael and Linda at the same time, all Buck could do was pray that all would turn out okay. Buck and Rachael stayed with Linda the rest of the day. Drinking coffee and pacing the hallway as well. Trying to be the moral support for Linda that she needed. A t about 3:00 pm the doctor came out of the operating room and met with all three of them. Dr. Higgins looked tired and worn out as he approached them, "We were able to stop the internal bleeding and no major organs were touched by the bullet. It's as if the bullet went out of its way not to hit anything important. We were surprised by the lack of damage done to him from the bullet. I think after a few days in the hospital he should be good as new."

With that, Linda started smiling, "When can we see him?"

"Maybe in a couple of hours when the drugs have worn off, he has lost a lot of blood so we have put him in a private room up on the third floor." Pointing at the lady sitting at the desk, "She should be able to tell you what room he's in. I must tell you he is one lucky man, I'll check on him in the morning."

The doctor left them to contemplate all that he had said. Rachael went to find out where the hospital had put Evans on the third floor.

As they made their way to the elevators the doors opened to let them in. When they reached the third floor the nurse's station was just off the entrance from the elevators. Linda asked the station nurse what room her husband was in, the nurse checking her charts, "Room 304." Linda headed there expecting to see him lying in the bed. When she saw that he had not arrived yet, she sat in one of the chairs in his room and waited for the nurses to bring him up from the operating room. Rachael stayed with her while Buck went to the nurse's station and asked when Evans would be arriving to his room. The nurse made a call down to post-op and asked when they could expect to bring the patient up to the third floor.

"He's being prepped right now, he should be up there shortly," the post-op nurse replied.

The floor nurse passed the message on to Buck, after which he went back to the room and told the girls, "Evans will be here shortly."

Linda and Rachael sat in the chairs watching TV but not seeing any of it. The shock of Evans being shot and coming out of it okay was still being registered in everyone's mind. Buck walked over to Linda, "What did you find when you were looking into Warren's bank accounts?"

It took a minute for Linda to come back into the real world before she could say anything to Buck.

"Our suspicions were correct about Warren, however, the money that came into his account was done electronically," She replied.

Buck thought on that for a moment, thinking that if you're transferring money to an account the last thing you want is a trail from where it came from. Buck looked at Linda, "Were you able to find out where it came from?"

"No, that's when Evans saw Warren and went after him, and now this."

"I'll go back to the bank and follow up on the trail of money being put into his account. Rachael will stay with you until I get back, alright?"

"Okay, just be careful, I can't afford to lose either one of you guys," Linda replied.

Buck walked out of the room and calling Rachael outside into the hallway he said, "You keep an eye on both of them, will you?"

Rachael nodded her head, "Buck, be careful out there, okay? I love you."

"I love you too, and I'll be careful."

Buck went back to the bank, identified himself, and asked one of the bank officers about Warren's account.

"Are you a friend of the FBI agent that was shot?"

"As a matter of fact, we are friends. I'm helping him since he's in the hospital recuperating."

"Is he okay? How is he doing?"

"He just got out of surgery, he's a very lucky man, he's going to be okay."

"Oh, that's good, tell him we wish him well."

The bank officer brought his account up on the computer screen, "I have the account up now, what would you like to know?"

"I need to know how many payments were made that were electronically sent into his account and where they came from."

"Give me a couple of minutes and I'll let you know."

As Buck sat there thinking about Evans being shot, he couldn't help but get angry for what a fellow FBI agent had done. He took his cell phone out and called Rachael, "Hey it's me, ask Linda about where Warren went after he was shot."

Rachael came back on the phone, "Linda doesn't know what happened to him. All she knows is that he was hit in the shoulder by Evans and after that he was gone. I'm sure Metro is looking into it to try and find him."

"Thanks Rachael, have you seen Evans yet?"

"Yes, he's here now and still sedated, but the color is back in his cheeks and he's resting comfortably right now."

"That's good news for everybody. I got to go, the bank officer has the information I asked for."

"Alright, I love you, see when you get back."

The bank officer was looking at the statements from Warren's account and had a puzzled look on her face. Buck seeing this asked, "What's up?"

The number of deposits all comes from a politician that hasn't been in office for years."

"Who is he?"

His name is Glenn Waters; he used to be the mayor of Las Vegas about five years ago. He was brought up on charges stemming from bribes he supposedly received from the syndicate while in office."

"What happened to him?"

"They couldn't prove anything. Although, right after that he resigned from being the mayor and was never heard of again as far as the political arena was concerned."

"Do you have an address for him?"

"Let me look for a second, yes here it is. It's 1221 Aspen Way, do you need to know where it is?"

"No, I already know where it is, thank you for your time. Would you do me a favor and send a copy of what you have there to the local FBI office, here's the address."

"Yes, I will be glad to and you're welcome."

Buck went back to the hospital and found that Evans was coming out of the pain killers and starting to make full sentences. Linda was seeing to his every need and Rachael just sat there watching the entire goings on with the nurses taking vitals and making sure Evans was comfortable. Buck walked in as the nurses were leaving the room and finding only Linda and Rachael there, he walked over to Evans, "You'll do anything to get out of work to talk to the nurses, won't you?"

Evans smiled and looked at Buck, "I bet you wish you were here instead of me?"

"No sir, with all the pretty nurses around here I'd get in trouble real quick. Besides, all of the attention around here would go to my head. So how are you doing?"

"I feel like I've been shot in the stomach, but considering all things I guess I'm doing better than I should be by all accounts."

"Considering how it could have gone, I'm thinking you're pretty lucky."

"I think you're right, Linda still won't let me play the lotto though. Who knows I could be rich and living the good life."

"I think you're lucky enough for me and my happiness," Linda said, reaching for his hand, and kissing it.

"See what I mean, all of this attention from the most beautiful women in the place and I can't help myself with her."

"Is there anything we can get you right now, either one of you?" Buck asked.

Evans and Linda shook their heads no. Linda, looking at them said, "Thank you for being here with us. I don't know what I would have done if you hadn't been here."

Rachael hugged her, "You just take care of that man there and that's good enough for us."

After leaving the hospital room, Buck and Rachael made their way back to the truck and sat there for a minute or two. Buck looked at Rachael, seeing she had tears in her eyes, reached over, and held her until the tears were gone. Buck knew it could have been any one of them that could be lying in the hospital bed hopefully recovering from whatever could have happened. He just held Rachael and kept saying, "I love you, it's alright, let it out."

Rachael let the flood gates open as she dealt with her own feelings of how important life is and how temporary it can be. Buck just held her and started to realize that life can have many twists and turns and we never know when its our time to go.

After about ten minutes Rachael regained her

composure and sat upright in the truck, "Did you find anything at the bank?"

"Yes, as a matter of fact I did, the old mayor of Las Vegas has the same address as our friend does at Mt. Charleston. And he's been paying Warren a lot of money over the years, for what I don't know yet."

"Well, where do we go from here?"

"I think we need to visit Ice Man again at his place of business and go from there."

"Let's ride over and take a look see. Should we visit the mayor while we're at it?"

"I think that's a good idea, let's go there first."

Buck started the truck and headed back to Mt. Charleston to meet the old mayor of Las Vegas. After a forty-five minute drive they were back at the house looking inside the windows again. This time there was no one around in the house. After opening the door, Rachael and Buck cleared the house and started nosing around looking for anything that would indicate any criminal activity. Rachael went into the bedroom and checked the closets and chest of drawers, carefully replacing everything back in its place after she was done searching. Buck kept a lookout for anybody coming towards the house. When they were done searching the house they made their way back to the truck and drove back to Las Vegas.

Buck was thinking while he drove back and finally asked Rachael, "Do you think we're looking at this the wrong way? Maybe the Ice Man is the mayor and he's running the show here in Vegas? The question is for whom is he running it?"

"I think this set up is too big for just for Ice Man alone. I think someone else is the boss and we need to find out who it is."

"I agree with you, the problem is, where do we start to look for the big players? I also agree that the mayor isn't acting on his own volition here. There has to be someone or some others involved."

"I think Evans might have been on the right track as far looking for the money source. Not so much Warren but who made the payments before the mayor started paying."

"Maybe we need to go back and look at the bank records again. I had the bank officer send it to the local FBI office here in town. The records should be there in the next couple of days."

"Let's stop by and see the kids maybe they know or heard something while they were there at the house," Rachael said.

They drove over to Gared's and Tina's house just in time for a snack from the kitchen. Miguel and Marissa met them at the door when they knocked. Marissa came running from the interior of the house and gave both Rachael and Buck a great big hug and wouldn't let either of them go as they made their way to the kitchen where everybody was eating. Miguel hugged his mom and dad and was leading the way. By this time Jennifer and Tim were up out of their chairs and hugging them as well. By the time Buck and Rachael seated themselves around the table they were inundated with questions from everyone wanting to know what was going on in the case of Ice Man and the others involved. Buck and Rachael sat there until they could answer each question with, "if I tell you I'd have to shoot you." Everybody laughed including Buck and Rachael. Finally, when everybody settled down Buck explained all that had happened up to this point, making sure he left out the bad stuff. It seemed to suffice for the group and everybody was just glad to see that everybody else was alright.

When he had finished eating, Buck asked the girls, "Do you remember hearing any conversations between the two guys that were guarding you, when they were in the front room?"

Marissa looked at Jennifer, "Not that I can recall." Jennifer nodded her head in agreement with Marissa.

"Did you have any visitors come by while you were there?" Rachael asked.

Marissa thought for a moment, "I remember one

of the guys calling somebody boss when he stopped by."

"How many times did he come by?"

"Two maybe three times."

"Do you remember what they talked about?"

"Something about a shipment coming in like before," Jennifer said

"Did they say when it was being shipped?"

Marissa jumped in and said, "Sometime this week."

Jennifer nodded again, "Yeah, this week."

Marissa started to think about the conversation, "Somebody big was coming in on this next shipment and they were worried about the loss of the last one you guys destroyed."

Buck looked at Rachael, "Looks like another all-nighter coming up for us."

Rachael asked Tina, "Do you have a thermos we can borrow for coffee and box for food we could use?" Tina sent Hannah down to the basement to fetch the thermos and a lunch box they could use.

Hannah thought that what Buck and Rachael were about to do was exciting, "Can I go with you guys?"

Tina looked at her, shocked that she would ask, "I don't think so."

To which Hannah stood there and asked, "But why mom?"

Buck looked at her, "Maybe next time you can go with us."

Hannah seemed happy with that and sat on the chair next to Tina. After getting the coffee poured into the thermos and sandwiches made and put into the lunch box, Buck and Rachael headed out the door and got into their truck and drove to the warehouse to begin their stakeout.

Chapter X

Warren was bleeding badly from the wound in his shoulder, the bullet passed through without hitting the bone. But the loss of blood made Warren feel faint; using his shirt as a bandage he was able to stem the flow of blood from the wound. Feeling better he moved to his car and got in to start it. His cover was blown as an informant for Ice Man. Now he needed to get to Ice Man to save his own life. Driving carefully so not to attract any undue attention, he carefully made his way to the warehouse where Ice Man would be. It was now 9:00 pm and this area of town was shut down for the evening.

The warehouse would have people inside even if Ice Man wasn't there. Warren had been there before, when he would pass information on to Ice Man, for the money, of course. Warren never cared much about the drugs, to him they were a crutch that weak people needed to use to get through life. Not Warren, he was strong he didn't need the drugs, all he needed was the money. He had keep the divorce from his wife quiet and by doing so he was able to keep any suspicion about himself away from anybody looking at his security clearance. The money started off as a loan to pay for the lawyers, but as time went on he couldn't or wouldn't give it up. He was in too deep to back out now; he crossed that line and lost all of his morals and values along the way. He blamed himself and also his wife for crossing the line and becoming a weak person to need the money now. For Warren, he had grown accustomed to the level of poverty he had attained and wasn't about to give it up.

All he had to do was look the other way and occasionally report where the FBI was looking for drugs, so that Ice man would know where to go and when to hide his drugs. As the drugs that were sold on the street increased, the money profit for Warren increased as well. Pretty soon he was making 1,000 dollars a week just by looking the other way. Warren figured he was making more by doing nothing than what the FBI was paying him to enforce the laws. Deep in his heart he knew that someday he would be caught and the price for crossing the line would come due, but in Warren's mind that was down the road, way, way, down the road. He said to himself, "If those damn kids hadn't been out there taking pictures this could have gone on till

I retired. Then I could go to some country down in South America and start over again, free from the Ice Man and away from my troubles with the FBI and ex-wife."

Warren's wife was always needing more money to gamble with, he had to mortgage the house twice to pay off her debts from gambling. Warren, at that time, decided to not give her any more money. This sent his wife into a downward spiral causing her to threaten to leave him and crying that she wouldn't gamble anymore, and would do anything to get the money she needed to pay off her debts. Warren stood firm, and after realizing he wasn't going to give her any more money, she walked out on him. Threatening everything she could think of to destroy him for not wanting to give her any money. Warren in the beginning would go out at night to try and find her but she was gone. And for him this nightmare was over and a new one was about to begin.

Having lost everything to pay off his ex-wife's gambling debts, he had nothing left in savings or his checking account. His house and retirement were gone and so was his wife. That's when he crossed the line, he was desperate to get back on his feet financially again, he would only do it a couple of times or so he thought, at least until he was on his feet again. One night, when he was driving home from work, there was his wife standing by the front door waiting for him. He asked her to come in and sit down. He was surprised to see her again. She was looking good for being out on her own and was dressed in high fashion clothes.

"So how have you been doing?" Warren asked.

"I'm doing fine, better than ever."

"What brings you here after all this time?"

"Well, I wanted to borrow some money from you again, seeing as how you're doing fine now."

Warren looked at her, shaking his head, "No, not again."

"Look, I only need 100 dollars then I'll be okay, and I promise you, I'll come home and be your wife again. We can start again just like new."

Warren slowly got up and opened the door, "You need to leave now."

"I see, you don't love me anymore, do you?"

Warren, taking her by the arm, took her to the door, "Don't come back until you don't gamble anymore," and shut the door behind her.

She stood there and pounded on the door until her hands hurt. She soon realized he wasn't going to change his mind and she turned away and never came back again. It wasn't until six months later, that they found her body in one of the back alleys of the hotels on the Strip. The coroner said, "It looked as if she had been beaten to death with a lead pipe."

Now, here he was waiting to go into the warehouse to get some medical help for his shoulder. He gave the customary knock on the door and went in. The guards looked at him, wondering what had happened to him. In a few minutes Ice Man showed up, "What happened to you?"

"I got shot by my boss."

"Why would he do that?"

"He saw me at the bank when I was trying to clear out my money."

"Why were you doing that?"

"They were on to me working for you; you gotta help me get out of Vegas."

Ice Man smiled, "I'll help you get out of Vegas."

With that he took out his gun and shot Warren in the head. He looked at his guys, "Get him out of here now."

Buck and Rachael heard the shot and instantly were watching the garage door to see what would happen next. In about five minutes, the door opened and the car carrying Warren headed off into the night. Buck decided to follow the car and within seconds he was following the it out into the desert. After letting them make the turnoff on a dirt road Buck switched off his lights and kept following the car. Seeing the brake lights come on he stopped his truck and he and Rachael both got out and walked to where the car was parked. The men were busy digging a hole for the body when Buck and Rachael got there. Spreading out in the darkness and drawing the guns, Buck yelled, "Freeze! And don't do anything stupid."

Both men being surprised, went for their guns and started firing. Rachael and Buck both fired their guns and both men went down. Rachael opened the trunk of the car and wrapped in plastic was the body of Warren. Buck came up to where Rachael was standing and looked in the trunk and closed his eyes for a second, then opening them again he said, "We need to call 911 and get this squared away."

When the police arrived on the scene Buck and Rachael, showing their badges, told the police what had happened. One of the detectives went over to look at the dead guys and said out loud, "Well, I'll be damned, look who this is."

The other detective came over to where his

partner was standing and looked down at the bodies, "I don't believe it, that's Jonesy from Ice Man's gang. Mr., you just did everybody a favor by taking this guy out as well as his partner. Jonesy here is wanted in at least two murders and we've been looking for him a long time now. You just saved the tax payers a lot of money for legal fees and prison time."

Buck smiled, "I didn't know who he was, all I know is he drew on me and I shot him to protect myself."

"Well, you did well as far as I'm concerned. Come on lets go home no use worrying about these two anymore. Oh, by the way, do you know the stiff in the trunk?"

"Yes, we do he was an FBI agent who worked here in Las Vegas. We'll take care of him ourselves," Rachael said.

The medical examiner called for a couple of ambulances to come and get the bodies of the three men to bring them back to his lab in Las Vegas, so he could perform autopsies on the bodies. Having found Warren's body in the trunk of the car would be enough to get a warrant to search the warehouse and arrest Ice Man for his murder.

The following day Buck and Rachael went to the hospital to share the news with Evans and

Linda.

"We found Warren, unfortunately so did Ice Man. We believe he was murdered by Ice Man. We caught up with two of his goons trying to bury the body out in the desert. We believe we have enough to indict Ice Man for his murder," Buck said.

"We now have enough to get a warrant to search his place and arrest him," Rachael added.

Both Evans and Linda were elated about Ice Man and in turn were sad about Warren being murdered.

"I will go down to US District Attorney this morning and get you a warrant for Ice Man's arrest," Linda said.

Buck and Rachael were excited to be able to go after Ice Man legally and stop him from doing anything worse than he was already doing. Too many murders outright and too many murders from the drugs he peddled on the streets in Vegas. This time the federal and state law enforcement units would be able to stop him in his tracks permanently.

Later that day, with the warrant in hand, Metro and Buck and Rachael raided his warehouse on West Flamingo Road and his house up on Mt. Charleston. Inside the warehouse they found the drug stash inside the locked room and assorted other items dealing with the drug delivery. The green van was sitting in one of the stalls inside the warehouse and with the pictures that Buck and Rachael had, it was enough to put Ice Man and his people away for a long time. The problem was Ice Man wasn't in either place; it was as if he disappeared into thin air. Now that the Feds and the local police were after him he was on the run, the problem was, where to look for him.

Earlier in the morning Ice Man received a phone call alerting him to the impending raid that was about to happen at the warehouse. He gathered all that he could and was out of the warehouse in five minutes. The raid was about hour later and he was already gone by then and on his way back to California. He knew his days were numbered in Vegas. Ice Man figured he would cut his losses and go back to Fresno and run his drug operations in Vegas from there. Ice Man had Tommy with him and two of his goons in the car as he left Vegas. Buck and Rachael were part of the raid at the warehouse; both were upset when Ice Man wasn't there to be arrested. Along with indictment, Buck had Ice Man's cell phone number traced, and all of his calls logged. Someone who had warned Ice Man about the raid worked in the Metro police department. They would be getting a visit from their superiors shortly about the phone logs showing the morning call that was made to Ice Man, along with a thorough background check on their own finances before being arrested.

Ice Man was a wanted fugitive, now on the run, and for all purposes he didn't have a place to hide no matter where he went. The U.S. Marshalls and other Department of Justice (DOJ) agencies would be after him now. Ice Man was furious that he had to move back to California and that he lost another load of drugs. He vowed he would get whoever had done this to him, and the worst of it was, would have to explain himself to his boss as to why he lost the business in Las Vegas. Ice Man was actually afraid of the boss man, he had seen his wrath or displeasure on the ones that were stupid. Right now, as he was thinking about leaving Vegas he had his goon, driving the car, stop at the small town of Good Springs, not only to refuel, but to get something to eat. As he leaned against the car, he thought about having to face the boss man, he didn't want to go back empty handed. Ice Man figured if he came back with who had done this maybe the boss man wouldn't be so upset with him. At that point, Ice Man told the driver, "Were going back to Vegas to find the man or men responsible for us having to leave Vegas."

As they turned the car around and headed back to Vegas, he called one of his friends and asked if he knew a place where he could hole up for a while. The friend told him of a place called Lathrop Wells, where he could stay without attracting attention. After hanging up, Ice Man told his driver to go to Lathrop Wells. Ice Man made another call to the boss man, "I'll be there in a couple of days to explain what happened. In the meantime, I've got some work to do first."

Having tapped his phone, the FBI now knew where the boss man was, and where to look for Ice Man.

Buck and Rachael were still in the hunt with everybody else looking for Ice Man. They drove up to Lathrop Wells and waited for Ice Man to show. Buck and Rachael figured they were ahead of Ice Man by about an hour, so they waited at the casino there along the highway, parked in the parking lot. The problem Buck and Rachael had was they didn't have a good up to date picture of what Ice Man looked like or, for that matter, what he was driving. The one that the FBI had was about two years old; hopefully he hadn't aged all that much during the last two years.

"So, what do you think of coming to Vegas for a vacation for a week or two?" Buck asked Rachael as they sat in the truck waiting.

Rachael looked at him, "Are you out of your mind?"

"I was just thinking we could go to Lake Mead and Mt. Charleston to ski and see Miguel and Marissa with the grand kids and all."

Rachael looked shocked, "Grandkids!? I'm not ready to be a grandma yet. And where do you get the idea that Miguel is going to marry Marissa? He barely knows her at all, besides I know he's not ready to get married yet."

"I was just asking what you thought about it all. I can't believe you, being an FBI trained profiler, you can't see what's in front of you. You must be getting old, you're at least 45 now, aren't you?"

Rachael, hit him, "You know better than that, I'm only 35 years old and I'm not ready to be a grandma yet. You're old enough to be a grandpa yourself you must be at least 40!"

"Yes, but I'm a sexy grandpa. You might say I'm a sexy senior citizen, heavy on the sexy part."

Rachael laughed even harder, "You're not sexy, and you're still a little kid."

"Whatever, I just want you to know the nurses

at the hospital were giving me the eye up there."

Now Rachael was really laughing, "You mean the old lady nurses?"

"Doesn't matter, because I'm a sexy senior citizen, and they love dirty old men."

"Well, you do need a bath and probably a shave too as well."

"Whatever you say, you sexy grandma you."

Rachael hit him again, "You really think I'm a sexy grandma?"

"Believe me, when I say you're a sexy looking grandma, I mean it."

After a couple minutes of sitting in the truck, Rachael looked over at Buck, "You really think Miguel is going to marry her?"

"You can see his eyes light up when she comes into the room when he's there. And she glows when he holds her hand."

"Wow, I never thought about them together like that. That does make me feel old now. If Miguel gets married and they have children that will make me the youngest grandma in the world."

"You're not old; you're like a bottle of wine that gets better with age, just like me."

"Nice recovery, you old wino."

"Thanks, I had to think fast on that one myself. Being as I'm a sexy senior citizen it's harder to do that lately."

By now, the sun was high in the sky and still no sign of Ice Man anywhere. Rachael decided that she was hungry, "You want to go in and get something to eat?"

"You know I'm kinda hungry myself, we old people need to eat more often than we used to when we were younger. I hope they serve Ensure in there," Buck replied.

"I'll get your cane or do you think you'll need your walker today?"

"Decisions, decisions, decisions."

When Buck and Rachael walked into the casino they headed over to the restaurant and got in line with the lunch crowd. The buffet was nothing to write home about, the typical buffet food was there, mashed potatoes brown gravy, macaroni and cheese for the kids Roast beast and fried chicken, the salad bar with all of the fixings and the dessert area with the chocolate fountain with the big marshmallows and cookies and cakes with the ice cream dispenser giving you two flavors or a twist. All in all, it was enough to keep you full while you were gambling. As they sat down to eat, the sound and smell of the casino was all around. If someone won on the slot machines the lights would start flashing and a siren would sound off. This was done to add excitement to the players inside the casino to entice them to put in more money in the machines they were playing. The cocktail waitresses would come around and ask the players if they wanted something to drink. They would quickly go get it for them and return with what the players had ordered as they spent their money in the machines. The card dealers were friendly at the 21 tables and would talk to you while they would deal the cards to you. The other table, with the spinning roulette wheel, was where the action was happening. Of course, that was the place where you could make or break your bank account. The smell of the stale cigarettes being run through the air conditioning system just added to the fun of the casino life. You could say this was life in the fast lane, all the glitter and noise with a chance to get rich in the game of chance. Inside the casino was always cool and little on the dark side for lighting. And with no clocks to be seen, the gamblers would never really know what the time of day it was. You could spend hours and dollars with no idea of what time it was and when you left the casino the light of the day would blind you and would take a minute or two to get your eyes acclimated to the light outside.

After eating the lunch buffet, they headed back outside to the truck to watch for Ice Man. As they were leaving the front of the casino, they saw Ice Man and his entourage walking into the casino. Buck tapped Rachael on the arm and nodded his head in the direction of Ice Man. Rachael looked in the direction that Buck had indicated and recognized Ice Man from the picture. She looked back at Buck and he motioned for them to go back outside.

After reaching the truck, Buck said, "It's better to wait for him outside than have a body count of innocents on our hands."

"I agree with you, should we contact the sheriff's department to let them know what's going on?"

"Not just yet, let's wait and maybe he'll lead us to another big fish in the pond."

As Ice Man sat down to have dinner at the buffet, his cell phone rang. Answering it, Ice Man stiffened when he realized who it was, and started saying, "Yes sir, I can handle this myself, you don't need to come out," and finally saying, "I'll pick you up at the airport outside, by the loading area for passenger pick up and drop off at 9:00 tomorrow morning."

After Ice Man hung up he was upset with the change of plans and swore under his breath. The boss man decided to come into Vegas to take a look see and figure what to do about the latest turn of events for Ice Man. He knew what this meant for him with the boss man showing up in Vegas. For him it meant pass, you live, fail, you die. At this moment, Ice Man wasn't sure he wanted to pick up the boss man at the airport tomorrow morning or just keep driving out of state. He had his money, approximately 50 thousand, in a brief case with him. He knew that would take him to Detroit and he could get lost in the city there. Maybe, starting up again as a drug dealer and working his way back to the top again. If he stayed to pick up the boss man, he would have to explain the loss of both drug shipments and the death of the FBI agent. Thinking about it, what could he say to the boss? Bad timing or being sold out by his informant, none of these excuses would appease the boss man and none would keep him alive after the meeting.

As he was thinking about this, a thought came to his mind, and it was a thought that might gain him more money than he lost in Vegas. He thought out load, "How about I take out the boss man and run the whole operation in California myself."

He then asked his guards, "Would you be

interested in making some money doing a hit for me?"

The guards nodded in agreement, "Who is the target?"

"I'll tell you later, not right now."

With that decision made Ice Man continued to eat his dinner without any interruption. When he was done eating, he and his two body guards went to their car and drove back to Las Vegas to wait out the night. Finding a cheap hotel to stay in, they spent the night close to the airport, and by 9:00 the next morning they were waiting at the curb for the boss man to show. When the boss man came out of the terminal he had two guys with him, all of them wearing suits and looking business like. Ice Man waved them down, and opening the trunk of the car had their luggage loaded into it. Boss Man rode in the back with one guy sitting next to him and the other guy up front with Ice Man.

Buck and Rachael were confused when they saw Ice Man leave the casino and head back to Vegas. Following him from a safe distance, they saw him stop at a hotel near the airport and spend the night.

At this point, Buck, not knowing what was going on, called Evans, "First of all, how are you doing?"

"I'm doing fine and getting stronger every day."

"I've got a problem and I need your input on this one. Ice Man drove back to Vegas last night and he's at the airport picking someone up. I think it's his boss and some of his goons from California."

"What makes you say that?"

"I saw Ice Man load the man's luggage into the trunk of his car. One of the men accompanying him, who look to be the boss, sat in the back of the car and the other sat up front with Ice Man."

"Sounds like it to me as well. Where are you now?"

"We are in Vegas following Ice Man."

"I'd say keep following him. Whatever you do, don't lose them."

"Rachael was able to get some pictures of the guy. I'll send you the pictures of him to your cell phone. That way Linda can run a face recognition program on him."

"I'll have Linda check the boss man out, good luck."

"Thanks, and get better."

Within minutes Linda, who was at the office, had the pictures and was running them on a face recognition program. It wasn't too long afterwards that the program came up with an identity for the face in the picture. Linda called Rachael, "The man in the picture is one of the head guys for the west coast operations for the drug cartel. His name is Manual Sanchez, a South American from Columbia with connections to one of the cartels down there. If we could capture him, and turn him, we would be able to possibly shut down the whole cartel operation on the west coast."

"I see, well I can't promise you anything, but we'll try and take him alive if possible."

Rachael looked at Buck, "You were right, we got a big fish on the line here."

"Tell me about him."

"He's from Columbia and he's in charge of the west coast distribution of drugs and Ice Man works for him."

"Oh goody, we get to nail both of them at once."

"We need to see if we can get the South American alive, if possible."

"You take all of the fun out of this don't you?"

"Yeah, that's why I never get invited to all of the parties anymore."

"I thought so, I didn't want to believe it, but after this, I guess it must be true."

Rachael and Buck continued to follow Ice Man

in their truck as they made their way on I-15 north bound to take the Flamingo exit to the warehouse where Ice Man had his base of operations set up. Seeing that the cops were still there, they drove by and continued to state route 95 to Lathrop Wells. After passing through Indian Springs, Buck and Rachael stopped to get gas for the truck and proceeded on from there. Catching up with Ice Man wasn't hard staying on the main route was the only way to Lathrop Wells unless you came through Pahrump. Staying close to Ice Man was easy especially when Rachael was using binoculars to follow him. Ice Man turned left onto Armargosa road and went into the valley to the place they would be staying at. The house was close by the Cherry Palace cat house. It wasn't much to look at as far as houses go, it was a vintage 1970s house with the same 1970s interior. It looked like it hadn't been lived in for quite a while. That being said, it met the needs of Ice Man for a place to hide out and the best part, no one would be asking any questions like why are you here and what are you doing.

Ice Man sat down in the chair in the front room, and the boss dusted off his chair before sitting down on it. Ice Man noticed that the two body guards were always with the boss. He smiled at this, thinking about the song that started out with "Me and my shadow. . . ." Ice man offered the boss a cold beer from the refrigerator as he got up to get one for himself. The boss accepted the offer and sat there drinking it. "So, tell me what happened out here with my drugs and my money?" asked the boss.

"We had some visitors a while back and they broke into the warehouse and destroyed my supply of drugs after tying up my guards first."

"Sounds plausible, did you catch the people who did this?"

"No, we don't know who they were."

"What about your FBI friend, he didn't know either?"

"He thinks it's a couple from Arizona that came up to help their son that we were following."

"Tell me about the boy you were following."

"On one of the nights we had air delivery and some kids took pictures of us unloading the drugs into the green van. We were able to find out who the kids were and started following them to get the pictures back. The boy who had taken the pictures had a friend. After the boy got away from us we thought we would follow the friend and see if he would lead us to the boy who had the pictures. We tracked the boys to the apartments they were living in and somehow or another they slipped out into the darkness and we lost them from there."

"The boss looked at his bodyguards and then looked at Ice Man, "You got your picture taken while unloading an airplane full of drugs, my drugs?"

Ice Man started to get nervous and looked at the floor, "We caught their girlfriends and had them in my place in Mt. Charleston to make a trade for the pictures. But they were taken from us by, we think, the same couple from Arizona."

The boss looked at his hands and his face started turning red with anger yelling, "So let me get this straight, you not only lost my drugs but you got your picture taken by some kids and on top of that you lost the hostages as well!?"

"Yes, I did, but I've never…"

"Tell me why I shouldn't kill you right here right now!? You have screwed up my entire operation here in Nevada and you have nothing but excuses for it!"

Ice Man tugged on his ear and both of the bodyguards dropped to the ground dead. The boss being surprised by this turn of events, stood there looking at Ice Man, who by now had a gun in his hand. The boss looked at Ice Man, "You wouldn't dare kill me."

By now the goons working for Ice Man made their appearance in the house, keeping the boss under surveillance as Ice Man began to speak. "I know you think I won't kill you, but I will, if you give me a reason to do so. I don't know where to find these two people who have stuck their noses into my business, but I swear, I will find them and kill them both."

While Ice Man was talking to the boss, Rachael and Buck found the car that belonged to Ice Man. Parking their truck a short distance away, they made their way to the house. Buck cased the house while Rachael provided cover for him as he went from window to window, checking to see what was inside. Finding Ice Man, with the boss inside, with his two bodyguards, proved to be a problem for Buck in taking out Ice Man. Carefully making his way back to where Rachael was he said, "We found the right place and everybody is in there. The problem is the two guards and Ice Man have guns on the boss right now. If we go in with our guns blazing, one of the bad guys is going to get shot and maybe us."

Rachael looked at him, "How about we do the same thing we did when we rescued the girls on Mt. Charleston."

"There has to be a way to draw them out of

the house without getting anybody killed, except for the ones we want dead."

"How about we shoot Ice Man's car or maybe shoot the tires out, that should bring the guards out of the house."

"Maybe we just knock on the door and as they open the door we shoot the guards and get the gun away from Ice Man."

"Works for me, but you get to knock on the door."

"Wait a minute."

Buck went over to the truck, grabbed a rag, and brought it over to the car. Opening the gas cap, he stuffed the rag into the opening and lit the rag on fire. Running for cover to the side of the house, they waited for the explosion from the car. Rachael set herself behind the opposite side of the house and waited as well for the explosion. When the car exploded all of them came running out of the house wondering what happened. Ice Man, looking at his car on fire and leaving a trail of smoke in the sky, just stood there shocked by what he saw. The two guards were quickly taken out, and that left Ice Man and the boss standing there. Buck yelled, "Ice Man, put the gun down now, or I will shoot!"

Ice Man, upset about losing his car, turned to fire at Buck, but as he was thinking about firing,

Rachael yelled from behind him, "Don't even think about it Ice Man!"

Ice Man dropped the gun and just stood there, waiting with the boss man with their hands in the air. Buck came over, kicked the gun away from Ice Man, and zip tied their hands together and marched them to their truck. Once Buck got them loaded into the back of the truck he then zip tied their feet as well. Buck got in and started the engine, took hold of the steering wheel pointed it in the direction of Las Vegas and started driving down the highway with Ice Man and his boss in the bed of the truck.

Rachael called Linda, "We got Ice Man and the boss man, where do you want us to take them?"

Linda was surprised by the phone call, and thought for a moment, "Take them to Metro for lockup and I'll meet you two there."

Linda called Metro police department and let them know that Ice Man and the boss man were coming in from the desert and to be ready to lock them up for the FBI. The metro officer that took the call wasn't sure what to do, so he called for the watch commander, "I just got this phone call from the FBI, informing us that they were bringing in Ice Man, and his boss. They are coming in from Lathrop Wells and they are asking us to lock them up in our jail."

The watch commander stood there, dumfounded for a moment, "I better tell the big boss about this."

Picking up the phone he called the police chief's office, he relayed the message to his secretary about Ice Man, and the boss man, coming in and that the FBI needed a place to lock them up in their jail. The police chief's secretary took the message and passed it onto the chief. Reading the note, the chief got up from his desk and walked down to the watch commander's desk and they both went to the front doors of the building waiting for Ice Man and the boss man to show. While they were waiting for them, Linda showed up, flashing her badge. She repeated the request to the chief about needing a place in their jail for Ice Man and the boss man.

When Tommy heard about Ice Man being captured by Buck and Rachael he started pacing in the hotel room he was staying in. Tommy knew he had to do something to save Ice Man. But when and where would it be? He also knew he was the only one left to do it. That was fine with Tommy, he had done things by himself before. He had to be patient and very quiet and when nobody was expecting anything, then he would save Ice Man from the bad people.

Tommy wondered what kind of surprise Ice Man would have for him when he saved him? Until then, Tommy knew he had to be patient and bide his time to save his friend.

Chapter XI

Linda showed up at Metro police department and by now the police chief, the watch commander, and at least ten other police officers were present when Buck and Rachael showed up in their truck. Both Ice Man and the boss man were completely docile. The police officers pulled them out of the back of the truck and stood them up after cutting the zip ties on the feet. Both men were asking for water when they were able to speak. Linda looking at the two men asked, "What happened to them?"

"I guess the hour ride in the back of the truck at 100 degrees took the fight out of them," replied Buck.

"This heat tends to do that to people, doesn't it?" Linda said.

By now, the officers had the two men in regular handcuffs and were escorting them to the jail cells waiting for them. The police chief came over to where Linda and Buck were standing, "Where did you find these two characters?"

They were sitting in a house in Armargosa Valley talking about Ice Man's bad luck when it came to his drug operations and his car," said Buck.

By now, Rachael was getting out of the truck, "You might want to call the Nye County sheriff's department and let them know about the bodies of the guards inside the house and outside as well. Just tell them to follow the smoke signal from the burning car we left for them."

The police chief, looking at the watch commander, nodded to him and with that the watch commander took off to take care of it. The police chief looking at all three of them asked, "Who is the second man with Ice Man?"

"The second man is Sanchez, he's from South America and runs the west coast distribution of drugs for the cartels in Columbia," replied Linda.

"Ice Man is also responsible for the murder of one of our FBI agents and trying to bury him out in the desert," Rachael added.

"Check your meat locker at the morgue. We will be glad to testify in court if necessary against Ice Man for the murder of Special Agent Warren," Buck interjected.

Linda walked over to the police chief, "Please don't let the press know we have Sanchez just yet, least wise until we talk to him first."

"Okay, that's fine by me, when do you want to interview him? What about Ice Man?"

"Most likely tomorrow after he recovers from the road trip that he had today. Ice Man will be brought up on federal charges for murder and possession of drugs with intent to sale and distribute, kidnapping, and last but not least, assault and battery."

"Works for me, seeing as how you feds found both of them, we'll let you guys handle all of it."

"That's fine, we'll get the U.S. attorney general to prefer charges against both of them. Hopefully, we can get them arraigned by next week. You might want your county or city attorney to sit in with our team and maybe come up with more charges from the city or county perspective."

"Okay, I'll get in touch with our city prosecutor and we'll go from there."

With that done, Linda went back to the hospital with Buck and Rachael to tell Evans the good news about capturing Ice Man and boss man. On the way there Linda said, "You know by now that the word of the Boss man being held in jail has already spread around the city and probably already on the west coast as well."

Buck nodded his head, "Yeah, I'm sure it

already has. We better be careful from this point on and watch each other's back until the boss man goes to prison."

"I'm worried about Evans being stuck in the hospital while all of this is going on. Someone could find out that he's in here and try to kill him or kidnap him and hold him hostage in return for the boss man."

"Maybe we could get him moved into a more secure place while we put boss man and his lackey in prison," said Rachael.

"It just depends on the doctors opinion as to whether we can move him or not."

They reached the hospital and made their way up to the third floor and stopping at the nurse's station. Linda asked the nurse on duty "Has the doctor had been up to check on Evans yet?"

She looked at the chart for Evans, "No not yet, it looks as if he may be running a little late today."

"Thank you."

Linda headed into Evan's room and saw that Buck and Rachael were already in there talking to him. Linda walked over and kissed Evans, "We got some good news for you."

"What's that?"

"Buck and Rachael here caught not only Ice Man but Ice Man's boss and drove both of them in the back of their pickup truck all the way from Lathrup Wells."

"No kidding, how did you guys get that done?"

"If we told you, we would have to shoot you again," Buck replied smiling.

"On no, not that again, once is enough for me."

"We caught them up in Armargosa Valley hiding out in a safe house that wasn't too safe for them. The worst part for them was the drive back in the back of our pickup, 75 miles per hour at 100 degrees and no shade. Although I have to say we were comfortable inside the cab of the truck with the a/c on. We kept hearing noises coming from the back of the truck so we had to keep turning up the radio on the way home."

Evans chuckled when he heard this from Buck. Linda added, "We have them in lock up at Metro police department, awaiting their charges and court dates. The attorney general and his staff will be working overtime on it for us and will try to expedite the process in order to get it done quicker."

"That's really good news."

"We thought you would like to hear some good news for a change of pace. So, has the doctor said anything about going home soon?"

"I'm hoping to hear today if, and when, I can go home."

After another 15 minutes of shooting the breeze, the doctor came in and, looking at the chart, asked, "So how are you feeling today?"

"Like a caged cat pacing in his cell, that's how I feel doc." The doctor was still looking at the chart when the nurse came in. The doctor looked at the nurse and asked if the pills were working for the patient.

The nurse, smiling, replied, "So far so good. This patient is not a very patient patient."

"Oh, come on now, I've been good. I've only thrown the bed pan once today. That's better than the three times I threw it yesterday, besides I think I pulled a muscle in my arm throwing it yesterday."

The doctor smiled, "How about we send you home on hospice tomorrow, would that work for you?"

Both Evans and Linda's eyes lit up, and both of them said, "Yes." at the same time. "The only problem we have is that we're staying in a hotel room right now."

"Not to worry we have a place for you to stay and recover. The food is real good there, as well. And you'll have 24/7 care while you're recuperating," Rachael stated.

"Nurse, get this bum out of here, we have real patients that need this room. We can't have him hurting his other arm throwing the bed pan, he might sue us," said the doctor, smiling.

As the doctor and the nurse left the room to get the paperwork started and squared away for Evans release, there was a sigh of relief from everybody in the room.

Linda looked at Buck and Rachael, "I will call you when were ready to leave tomorrow morning. Just out of curiosity, where are we going to be taking Evans to?"

"Not to worry, it's a safe place for him to heal up and nobody knows about it, that's the best part of it all. We need to go and prepare the family for their new guests," Rachael said.

Buck and Rachael said their goodbyes and left the hospital and headed back to Gared and Tina's place to let them know who was coming for a long visit. Unbeknownst to them, they were being watched from another car in the parking lot. The two men in the car were undercover cops watching out for anybody that might be following Buck and Rachael's truck. Their job was to ensure that Buck and Rachael were there to testify against Ice Man and the boss. You could say that Buck and Rachael were in the witness protection program without their knowledge. As the two men pulled out of the hospital parking lot they followed Buck and Rachael's truck to the Gared and Tina's house. Keeping a safe distance from Buck and Rachael, they parked up the street to keep an eye on them and from being spotted by either Buck or Rachael. When they got inside the house Buck and Rachael talked to Gared and Tina about Evans.

"Evans is recuperating from a sickness, and being from out of town, he needs a quiet place to stay so he could heal and get better," Buck said.

"Not a problem, we have your old room he can have to recover in," Tina said.

"The problem is, we don't how long he'll need to stay here."

"And your point is?"

"You're good people and we really appreciate what you're doing and what you've already done," Buck said smiling.

"Where is Miguel, is he here?" Rachael asked.

"He's in the TV room watching TV with Marissa."

Buck and Rachael made their way to the TV room and found Miguel, sitting next to Marissa, asleep on the couch. Buck looked at Rachael and pointed to Miguel and Marissa as they slept on the couch. Rachael smiled at them, "They make a lovely pair together, don't they? I hate to wake them up."

Buck gently tugged on Miguel's shirt until he awoke. Once Miguel was able to see who it was, he smiled, and standing up, he hugged both Buck and Rachael for a minute.

"I am so glad to see you guys, where have you been?" Miguel asked.

Buck whispered, "We have a favor to ask of you. Do you remember Evans and Linda, the people you stayed with until we got back from Columbia?"

"Yes, I do."

"Well, they're both here working with us on this drug case and Evans is coming here to recover from a gunshot wound. We need you to keep an eye on him so that nothing happens to him while he is here."

Miguel was excited to see Evans and Linda again, and was excited to be needed to assist Evans in his recovery. "Consider it done," Miguel said.

"However, you can't tell anyone about the how he got hurt okay? For all we know, there may be bad guys out there looking to hurt him again."

Miguel nodded, "What wound?"

Buck and Rachael smiled at Miguel and

hugged him again, this time Rachael said, "You guys look good together," pointing at Marissa. To which Miguel turned red in the face and was speechless.

Buck laughed, "Your mother, always the match maker in the family."

Buck and Rachael left the house and went back to their motel room to get some sleep. Buck was thinking that with Ice Man in jail and the boss man with him, he thought about returning to Arizona to being a sheriff once again. Looking at Rachael he said, "What do you think about going home soon?"

Rachael nodded, "That would be nice. What about the court and the arraignment?"

"We can come back up for that if necessary."

"Let's ask Linda, after we get Evans taken care of first."

"Sounds good to me. I'm ready to go home, this town of Las Vegas is too big for me."

The next day came with the phone ringing, it was Linda calling to tell Buck and Rachael that she was ready to take Evans to Gared and Tina's house. Rachael and Buck were on their way in about 30 minutes. Meeting them at the front of the hospital, Buck and Rachael helped Linda put Evans into the car that Linda was driving. Rachael offered to drive Linda's car to Gared and Tina's place, just for ease of getting there. Buck followed in the truck right behind them, and as they were making their way down the street, there was some road construction going on up ahead. Rachael stopped Linda's car for the work zone. Rachael noticed that the one of the flagmen seemed a little over dressed for the job.

Rachael called Buck on the phone, "I don't like this; it doesn't feel right to me," she said nervously.

Buck jumped out of the truck and started walking forward having drawn his weapon and using the cars as a shield to get to Rachael and Linda. By now, Linda and Rachael both had their weapons drawn and down at their sides, looking for anything not right. Buck was now alongside their car, watching the road crew workers. About that time, the flagman reached beneath his vest and pulled his gun out, getting ready to fire. Buck dropped him with one shot to the chest, the other road crew members pulled their weapons as well. With the flagman down Buck told Rachael, "Get out of here now."

Rachael gunned the motor and ran over the flagman and hit one other guy as she made her way out of the construction zone. Buck kept the other road crew members pinned down firing his weapon from behind the road crew truck until the Metro police department officers showed up.

The man that had been hit by Rachael's driving was laying on a gurney waiting for the ride to the hospital. Buck went over and asked the man, "Who sent you?"

"Nobody sent me," barely able to say the words because of the pain.

"The sooner you tell me, the quicker you can go to the hospital," reaching over to the man's leg and grabbing it.

The man let out a scream for the pain that Buck introduced him to, and in between breaths the man said, "Sanchez sent us."

Buck released the man's leg, enabling him to start breathing normal again. "How much was Sanchez willing to pay for the hit?" grabbing the man's leg again.

Another scream, and the words came out, "50,000 dollars" the man said.

Sobbing because of the pain and with his grip still on the leg, Buck looked at him with steely eyes and squeezing harder asked the man, "Was it worth it?"

This time man was pleading for Buck to release his grip from his leg. One of the Metro officers came over and said to Buck, "Look I understand why you feel the way you do, but people are starting to show up and you and I don't need that right now."

Buck released his grip on the leg and the man was still gasping for breath because of the pain that had been inflicted by Buck. At this point the man was loaded into the ambulance and taken away.

Buck, looking at the officer, "He tried to kill my wife and our friends."

The cop looked at Buck, finally understanding why Buck was being such a hard case to the man, "He won't leave Vegas in one piece when it comes time for him to leave."

Rachael finally slowed down about a block away from the intersection continually checking her rear-view mirror and looking for cars that could be part of the attempted hit. Seeing nothing, she continued to Gared and Tina's place, driving around the block a couple of times to make sure there were no people in the parked cars in the area she stopped in front of the house. Quickly taking Evans on one side with Linda on the other side they half carried Evans into the house. Tina opened the door to let them in, she saw the look of intensity in both of their faces and knew something had gone wrong. Linda, with the assistance of Miguel, helped Evans into the bed Tina had set up for him.

Once he was safe in bed, Evans said to Linda, "Let me have your gun for protection while I'm staying here."

Linda gave him her gun, "I'll get your gun and bring it to you when I get the chance to do so."

By now, Rachael's phone rang and it was Buck on the other end, "First of all, are you guys alright?

"Were okay," she said excitedly. "How about you, are you okay?"

"I'm fine, where are you at?"

"We're at the house," she said, trying to calm down. Evans is already upstairs in bed.

"Anyone follow you there?" Buck asked urgently.

"Not that we could tell, we went around the block a couple of times to make sure we weren't being followed, didn't see anyone," she said, finally being able to compose herself once again.

"Good, I'll see there in a minute or two," Buck said, as the adrenaline started to wear off.

Getting back into the truck, Buck drove off in the direction of the house; the two police officers who were tailing him didn't say a word to each other as they continued to follow his truck. Both of them knew they had screwed the pooch on this one, and both of them knew there would be hell to pay for this screw up by the end of the shift.

Linda came down the stairs, looking nervous, asking Rachael. "Is Buck okay?"

"He's fine and is on his way here," replied Rachael.

Linda, looking relieved, sat down on a chair in the front room trying to collect her thoughts and Rachael coming over said in a playful manner, "You know what they say about Vegas don't you?"

Linda looked at her for a minute trying to figure out what she was asking, and laughed out loud, "What goes on in Vegas, stays in Vegas."

"Damn Skippy," she said, laughing out loud as well.

Chapter XII

Buck showed up at the house, and looking around, made sure he wasn't followed either. By now, everybody was in a good, but guarded mood. Tina knew well enough not to ask about what happened earlier. She and Hannah started to make dinner for everybody and was busy slicing the tomatoes for the salad she was preparing. Hannah had been introduced to Evans and Linda already, and knew her job was to make sure that Evans was taken care of. At first, Hannah wasn't excited by the new job, but once she found out that Evans was a big time FBI agent from Washington D.C., she quickly decided this wasn't too bad of a job to have. Linda was upstairs with Evans keeping him company, and as she closed the door behind her she saw Buck standing at the bottom of the stairs. She went down the stairs and ran over and gave him a great big hug and a kiss on the cheek. "That's for saving us today, they had us cold. If you hadn't been there I don't what would have happened to us," she said tearfully.

"You're welcome and maybe I ought to do this more often," Buck said, surprised by all of what just happened.

"You do it again and I'll let them shoot you myself," Rachael said, jokingly.

"Yes ma'am, three bags full ma'am," Buck said, obediently.

Everybody laughed at the comments and life went back to normal. Buck asked about Evans and Linda replied, "He's asleep right now. The trip wore him out more than he could handle. With all of the excitement, he's still weaker than he'd like to admit."

"At least he's safe and sound," said Buck.

After dinner, Buck approached Linda about talking to her privately. Linda met Buck and Rachael in the den, "What's up?"

"We were thinking that it was about time for us to head back to Arizona," Buck said.

"What did you say," Linda said in a surprised tone.

"We were thinking that it was about time for us to be heading back to Arizona," Buck said, hesitantly repeating himself.

"I thought that's what you said," Linda said catching her breath. She continued, "You can't leave right now, especially with Evans still recovering. I can't do this alone, at least not right now," she stammered.

"That's why we wanted to talk to you first. We have been up here for a week now and we feel like we've done all we can do, with the exception of the court testimony and such," Rachael said softly.

Linda, looking down at the floor in the den, thought for a minute before looking into the eyes of Buck and Rachael with understanding, "I understand how you feel about being away from home. Lord knows I feel it too, being here instead of Washington. Being out here, living in a hotel in Vegas, and having Evans shot, has made it hard for us too. I also understand that you have your jobs waiting for you, as well. But right now, I really need you two to be here with me, there is no one else I can trust to back me up here."

"Enough said, we will stay as long as you need us to," Buck said with a determined voice.

Rachael nodded her head in agreement, "We're in this together to the end."

Buck and Rachael left the house right after checking on Evans, making sure he was good and comfortable. As they drove back to the hotel they were staying in, a car drove up alongside of them and paced them with the passenger rolling down his window and firing his weapon into the truck. Buck slammed on the brakes and took the first left to lose the car. However, the second car saw the move and pulled in behind them and gave chase down the street. One of the bullets had hit the engine block and the truck started to slow down losing water, with steam pouring out from under the hood. The car was right there on top of them, with the second car closing in as well. Buck and Rachael, not hit from the first attempt pulled their guns, jumped out of the truck, and waited until the first car was close enough. They then fired into the windshield of the car taking the driver and the front passenger out. The two men in the back were getting out of the car when they starting firing their Uzis. The machine guns raked the full length of the truck as Buck and Rachael lay on the ground with their guns raised and waiting for the two to show their faces. Just as they came from around their car, Buck and Rachael fired into both of them. By now the men in the second car were making themselves known by firing at Buck and Rachael. Buck looked at Rachael, "I'm running low on ammo, how about you?"

"I'm down to my last clip as well," Rachael replied.

As they lay there on the ground, they could hear other shots being fired, and one of the men from the second car fell to the ground. The others, with the fallen man, stopped their forward progression, turned around, and started firing behind them. Buck and Rachael seeing this got up and started firing into the group of men as well, taking two more out. As they hit the ground, the fourth man threw his gun down on the ground and raised his hands above his head. A man's voice could be heard telling the fourth man, "Get down on your knees and put your hands behind your head."

The fourth man did as he was told, and another voice came from the shadows saying to Buck and Rachael, "Don't shoot, I'm coming out."

He then came out of the shadows and went over to the kneeling man and slammed him, face first into the pavement. After Buck and Rachael covered the man lying on the ground, the man from the shadows handcuffed him and picking him up took him to his car and put him in the back seat.

Buck and Rachael looked at the two men when they came back, "Who are you guys? And thanks for helping us."

One of the two introduced themselves, as Metro police department detectives, "We were assigned to look after you guys in case something like this happened. Oh, by the way, we're sorry about this morning when you guys ran into the other problem."

"All is forgiven, we owe you guys one," Buck humbly said.

"No, if anything were even now. Thanks for letting us rescue you," the detective said.

"Any time, any place. The only problem we have now is we're out of wheels and we need to get back to the hotel we're staying at," Rachael replied.

"I know someone who won't need their car anymore. The keys still should be in the ignition, why don't you take it for a test drive tonight and bring it back sometime tomorrow," the detective said.

"Works for me and the girl I go with," Buck said, smiling at the detectives.

"Jeez, you always say the sweetest things," Rachael replied.

"You guys have a nice night and drive safe, you don't want to get pulled over driving someone else's car," one of the detectives said chuckling.

"We'll take care of your truck and let you know where it is for pickup," said the other detective.

Getting in the car they noticed a slight smell of

marijuana in the car. "Oh great, now if we get pulled over their going to nail us for DUI," Buck said laughing.

Rachael laughed, "You know I could get used to this. You know what, all of a sudden I'm hungry now."

"Me too," Buck said, "Me too."

Buck and Rachael reached their hotel room after midnight, and falling into bed they slept all the way through till morning. After waking up, they took their time getting dressed. Going out for coffee and breakfast, they made their way to the local Denny's restaurant. Sitting inside one of the booths, they sat there talking about what Linda had said to them. "Do you realize we don't know where Jenkins is in all of this," Buck said.

"You know you're right about that, we haven't seen neither hide nor hair of him since Warren took off," exclaimed Rachael.

"Maybe we need to go and check his place out and look around a little bit."

"Okay, let's do that," Rachael said eagerly. "Besides, it'll give us something to do today."

After breakfast, they got into the car and drove to the police station to drop off the car with the detectives. The one detective, named Frank, said, "Thanks for bringing it back in one piece. Your truck is at Bill's towing service on Main and North Las Vegas Boulevard. Here is their number to call if you wish to find out about your truck."

"Thanks, but I think the truck has seen its better days now," Buck said, feeling kind of down about it.

"Cheer up we explained what happened to you last night to the tow truck driver and between him and Bill, they found another engine for your truck and will replace it free for you. They even have a loaner for you to drive till the truck is repaired," Frank said, beaming with good news.

"I don't know what to say, except thank you for helping us like this," Buck humbly said.

"Aww, don't think nothing of it, we just appreciate you two for capturing Ice Man and his boss for us. Do you need a lift to Bill's place to get the loaner car?" Frank asked.

"That would be greatly appreciated," Rachael said.

After being introduced by Frank to Bill, as the owners of the truck that he had in his shop, Bill shook both of their hands, "I'm so glad to meet you two, thanks for stopping Ice Man for us."

"I don't understand what all the hoopla is all about," said Buck.

"It's like this; my son was killed in a drive-by, by the guys that work for Ice Man. He was coming home one evening with some friends and a car drove by thinking that the group of kids were part of a gang, they came around again and were shot by the passengers in the car. After the cops did the investigation, it was found out that Ice Man ordered the hit, thinking they were competition from out of town."

"We are so sorry for your loss," Buck said quietly.

"Ice Man got off on a technicality, and the witnesses they had, refused to testify against him out of fear. Seems he found out who was on the jury and sent flowers to each of the witness's houses as a threat not to talk," Bill said, still upset about it.

Buck and Rachael didn't know what to say, from that point on all they could do was thank him for working on their truck.

"Think nothing of it; you guys have done what nobody else has been able to do by getting that scumbag off the street. I know it won't bring my son back, but it will keep somebody else's parents from having to go through what I have gone through," Bill's face brightened as he said that.

Rachael came over and gave Bill a hug,

"Thank you Bill, for restoring my faith in good people, they are still out there and your one of them."

Bill looked away and started wiping his eyes, "Damn allergies."

Buck and Rachael smiled, as did Bill as he threw some keys at them, "It's the red car out there, give me a couple of days before you come back, salright?"

"Salright," Buck replied.

As Buck and Rachael drove off in the red car Rachael laid her head on Buck's shoulder and left it there until they got to the FBI office. When they walked into the office they could see Sherron was back at her desk and typing on the keyboard of her computer. She looked up, "Can I help you?"

"Is Linda in the office?" asked Rachael.

"Just a moment," said the secretary as she rang her office. The secretary said over the phone, "There are two people here to see you."

Linda came out, "Well, what do you know, the people you run into with guns around here, of all the places," she said joking. Before Buck or Rachael could say anything, Linda looked at Sherron, "Do you know who these two are?"

"I remember seeing them before my accident but I can't recall your names," she said trying to remember them.

"These two were the ones that found you lying on the floor the day you got hurt."

With that, Sherron stood up and came from around her desk and hugged both of them. "You saved my life that day, and I will never forget you for that," she said, with a thankful heart.

"You're more than welcome, and how are you doing?" said Buck happily.

"My head still hurts once in a while, but it's getting better day by day, nothing that a good strong aspirin won't cure," she said.

"Glad to hear that," said Rachael.

By now, Linda motioned the two of them into her office and shut the door behind her. Looking at both of them, "What can I do for you two today?" she cheerfully asked.

"We were wondering about Jenkins and his whereabouts?" said Buck "Do you think he was part of the problem here or an innocent bystander?"

Linda lowered her head, "That we may never know. We found his body yesterday afternoon near where you found Ice Man's goons digging a hole for Warren," she said sadly.

"Wow," said Rachael. "How did it happen?"

"Shot in the back of the head twice, near as we can tell anyway," Linda said, in a matter of fact voice. She continued, "It looks like a professional hit."

The news stunned both Rachael and Buck, and as they sat there taking it all in, Linda's phone rang. When she answered it the voice on the other end told her the arraignment for Ice Man was going to be today at 3:00 pm in the federal court house.

"Thanks for the update, we'll be there," Linda said.

Linda looked at Buck and Rachael, "You want to go to Ice Man's arraignment today?"

Buck and Rachael smiled, "Wouldn't miss it for the world. When and where is it?"

"Today, at three in the courthouse, on the third floor," she said excitedly.

"Finally, we get to see the fruit of our work come to a completion," Rachael said looking at Buck.

Tommy, looking at the court schedule on the bulletin board, could see that the arraignment for Ice Man was today at 3:00 pm in number two court. Tommy made his way to the court and sat down waiting for the bad people that were holding Ice Man to come in. As he sat there, he was very quiet, and therefore, he was not questioned or anything. He just sat and waited for Ice Man to show.

Later that day, Buck and Rachael were sitting in the courtroom on the back row. They were watching the proceedings, with Linda sitting at the federal attorney's desk in the front of the courtroom. Unbeknownst to anybody in the room, Tommy was sitting right behind the federal prosecutor's desk. As he sat there waiting, the prosecutor stood up ready to justify federal government's position for no bail for Ice Man. As Buck and Rachael watched the legal system do its part with the two attorneys justifying their positions regarding the bail for Ice Man. All at once, Tommy, who was sitting in the courtroom, jumped up over the railing and ran towards the prosecuting attorney and tried to tackle him to the ground. The attorney hit his head on the desk and was knocked out cold. Linda was thrown to the side of the desk and was pinned under the attorney. The bailiffs tried to get Tommy off of the two of them. Using their stun guns, they were able to drag him off of Linda and the attorney. However, the stun didn't stop Tommy from attacking the two bailiffs. Buck jumped up and tackled the guy to the ground taking the bailiffs with him. Tommy grabbed one of the bailiff's guns and was raising it up to shoot the judge. By then, Rachael had her gun out and shot Tommy twice in the back.

It was as if the bullets didn't have any effect on him. As he continued to raise his gun, Buck, who was still on the ground, kicked his knee and Tommy went down firing his gun hitting the dais that the judge was sitting behind. This time one of the bailiffs pulled his gun and fired twice into Tommy while he was on the ground. Both shots hit him in the chest, he tried to get up, and calling out Ice Man's name, he fell back and died.

Ice Man came running over and knelt down, and said, with tears in his eyes, "Tommy, Tommy, you didn't have to do this."

The bailiffs grabbed Ice Man and set him back down in the chair on his side of the courtroom.

The judge, having witnessed all of this, taking his seat, slammed the gavel down, "Bail denied!"

At this point, the court was adjourned while the EMTs were brought in to take care of the federal prosecutor and Tommy.

Linda, picking herself up, smiled at Buck and Rachael, "Well, that was fun, I wouldn't have missed it for the world."

Buck and Rachael laughed as all three of them walked out of the courtroom.

Later that night, at Gared and Tina's house, Linda and Rachael were telling what had transpired during the day.

Evans shook his head, "You guys have all the fun! And I'm here with this measly hole in my stomach with nothing to do."

"Next time we'll take pictures and bring them home, so you can see them, and Buck will do the narration," Linda laughed.

"It's better, but nothing like the real thing," He smirked.

Chapter XIII

The driver stood, leaning against the wall, waiting patiently for the bus to park so that he could see if the two men he was waiting for were on it. He was told via a phone call that the two men would be arriving by bus from California and coming to Vegas. Hoping this was the bus, he stood there watching the passengers get off. As another bus pulled in next to the bus he was watching, the two brothers who were sitting in separate seats got up to leave the bus. As the people filed off of the bus, the driver recognized them and waved as they stood waiting to pick up their luggage.

The driver walked up to them and shook their hands, "Glad you could make the trip, how was the drive up from California?"

"Uneventful, did you bring what we requested?" One of the brothers said.

"Yes, it's in the trunk of the car, just like you asked for," the driver said.

Not being seen, was another man who had been there watching the people getting on and off the buses, as well. His job was to keep an eye on passengers that were not your typical riders. The poor people who were visiting families and people looking to make a brand-new start in Vegas. His main concern was the kids who were running away from home, hoping to make it big, working on the Strip. These he watched for, most of all, trying to get them before the pimps did. For the most part, he was successful, other times he wasn't. Being only one of two plain clothes police officers working the bus depot, he needed his days off like any other worker.

As he watched the two men get off the bus, he realized that these two were not your typical riders. By looking in their eyes, he could tell they were bad news. Their eyes were cold and distant and had no feeling of warmth in them. Discreetly taking their pictures, he moved on to the next bus that was coming from Phoenix and started watching the people getting off of that bus. After the two men left the depot with the driver he sent their pictures to the Metro police department identification section for face recognition, along with the license plate number of the driver's car. The plain clothes police officer had done his job now it was up to the computers to do their job.

As the driver took his passengers to their hotel

room he told them, "I will pick you up tomorrow morning at 6:00.

One of the brothers, looking at the driver, as he unpacked his clothes said, "That won't be necessary. We need to get our gear out of the trunk of the car."

The driver went with one of the brothers to retrieve the gym bag from the trunk of the car and helped with getting it into the hotel room. Inside the gym bag were the weapons they had requested for the hit. It was all there, just like the two brothers had asked for. One of the brothers asked for the keys to the car. The driver looked at him with a puzzled look on his face, handed the car keys to the brother. Standing there for a moment, the second brother came up from behind and with a quick movement sliced the driver's throat creating a happy face from ear to ear. Catching the driver as he fell to the ground, they dragged his body into the bathroom and put him into the tub, where he would bleed out without making a mess all over the bathroom floor.

The two brothers repacked their suitcases and left the hotel room with the driver's car and found another hotel to stay in. This was normal for the two brothers. This way, there would be no lose ends to tie them to anybody who could talk to the police and identify them in any way, shape, or form as to their purpose of why they were here. The driver's body would be found the next day by the cleaning maid but that would be enough time for them to do what they were here in Vegas to do and be on their way back to Los Angeles, this time flying.

The facial recognition software was loaded with the picture of the two men at metro and the computer went on a journey inside the memory banks looking for the two men. In about an hour, the computer found the men in its memory bank and sounded an alarm to let the computer operator know that it had done its job. The computer operator, looking at the pictures of the two men with their names at the bottom of the page, picked up the phone and called the man in charge of the Metro Intel Section to let him know they had a hit on the facial recognition software. The man on the other end of the phone was Mat, a ten-year veteran police officer who had been working in the Intel Section for the last three years. Asking the computer operator who the names were on the pictures, the operator said, "The Calderon Bothers from Los Angeles."

Mat just about dropped his phone, then regaining his composure asked, "Are you sure about that?"

The operator confirmed the names to Mat, "According to the information on the screen these guys are bad news."

"You don't say," Mat said cynically.

With this new information, Mat would send a message out through the intranet about the Calderon brothers being in Vegas arriving yesterday by bus. Mat thought for a moment, wondering what would bring the brothers here to Vegas. As he thought about it some more, it hit him like a ton of bricks. Running over to his computer he looked up the latest news about apprehensions being made in the local area. Sure enough, there it was, a short article about Sanchez being delivered by truck with Ice Man to Metro police department by two FBI agents. Mat quickly called his contact in the FBI office to relay the information he had received from their sources, saying there may be a possible hit on somebody here in Vegas, most likely the two FBI agents that had brought in Sanchez.

Linda, picking up the phone in her office, listened to the voice on the other end, then she quietly hung up the phone. Picking her cell phone up, she called Buck and Rachael. After the second ring, Buck answered the phone. Upon identifying herself she asked them to come back to the office for a minute.

When Buck and Rachael got to the office Linda called them in and closed the door behind her. Buck, sensing something wasn't right, did away with the pleasantries and sat down across the table from her, Rachael did likewise. Linda looked at them for a moment before saying anything, as if she was trying to find the words to start the conversation. After a minute Buck asked, "Okay, what's wrong Linda?"

"There are two men looking to kill you for capturing Sanchez, Ice Man's boss," Linda said nervously.

"Oh, is that all, well I thought it was something serious," Buck jokingly said.

"These guys are brothers and they are out of L.A .and they work for Sanchez, their names are Calderon. And from what I gather, they're considered to be real mean people," said Linda

"Do you know where they are at?" Rachael asked.

"Evidently, they came by bus from Los Angeles and were picked up by a man driving this car," Linda handed them a picture of the car. "We ran the license plate number and found it belonged to a Mark Lopez, who metro found in a bathtub dead in a hotel room yesterday. His car was gone and we assume the two brothers are driving it," Linda said. "Here are pictures of the two of them at the bus station."

After studying the pictures for a couple of moments, Buck set them down on Linda's desk.

"What kind of car is it?" asked Rachael.

"It's a gold 1963 Chevy Impala, 2 door hardtop lowrider," Linda replied.

"Wow, nice car, I used to own one of those a long time ago, at least Mark had good taste," Buck said, laughing.

Linda looked at him with a puzzled look on her face. "I take it this doesn't bother you at all," she said, questioning his joking.

"I'm sorry for not taking this serious; I have to say, we've been shot at twice no, three times by three different groups of people. We've had to shoot people to get information to find the girls and get Ice Man and Sanchez, and go to Frankie Diamond to call off a hit from the syndicate. Why should this be any different from the others that have tried?" Buck said emphatically to Linda. "It's all in a day's work here in Vegas for us."

Linda looked at Rachael, with her nodding back, "Ditto, is there BOLO out for the car right now?" Rachael asked

"Metro is looking for it as we speak, but no luck yet," Linda said, frustrated.

"Well one thing for sure, they'll be looking for

us, so we just have to be ready when they come for us," Buck said, in a matter of fact attitude. "Right now, we need to stay away from the kids so they don't get hurt, or for that matter Evans, as well."

Rachael looked at Linda, understanding her fear and frustration about the Calderon brothers, "It's alright we'll get through this, one way or the other."

"It's the other that worries me right now," Linda replied.

With that, Buck and Rachael left the federal building and headed to their red car, looking for a late model Chevy Impala. Linda stood up and watched Buck and Rachael make their way to their car through her office window. As she stood there, she picked up the phone and called one of the other special agents in charge into her office.

Linda looked at him, "You see that red car right there and the two-people getting into it? Your job is to make sure they don't get killed or it's your ass on the line. Take as many people as you need, but follow them wherever they go. Do YOU understand?"

"Not a problem, we're on it," the agent said.

Linda thought to herself, "I know that you guys can handle yourselves, but I want to know you're going to be okay, no matter what."

Within minutes, the FBI started trailing Buck and Rachael in their own car. Buck and Rachael were headed in no real direction as they drove through town unaware that the FBI was tailing them. The Metro detectives were not too far behind the FBI agents, and recognizing the crown Victoria as an FBI vehicle, kept their distance from them as well.

"Well what do you know, the FBI is on this one as well," Frank said to his partner.

For the rest of the day Buck and Rachael pretended to be tourists driving up and down the Strip, going out to Red Rocks State Park, and driving to Lake Mead to see Hoover Dam, all the while taking pictures of everything.

When the day was done, they headed back to their hotel room and went and picked up a Little Caesar's pizza for dinner. For the rest of the night they sat and watched TV for a couple of hours before going to bed. Shutting off the lights, the place was quiet, and for the most part, they had a good day seeing all of the sights around Las Vegas.

Not too far away, the FBI agents and Metro detectives settled in for a long night of another stake out. About three in the morning Buck woke up to a sound from outside the widow below him and got up to look outside to see where the noise was coming from. He saw the two detectives grabbing a man with a gun and quietly dragging him back to the car handcuffed. The FBI was down there as well, watching the show and cussing that they didn't get the guy first. Buck smiled and waved at the detectives down below and went back to bed.

The next morning was bright and already starting to get warm, not as warm as Phoenix, but pretty close to it. Buck reached over and woke Rachael up by kissing her on the forehead. She moved a little and grabbed Buck in a tight hold around his neck and kissed him back. "That'll teach you to sneak up me," she said playfully.

With that, the pillow fight started and didn't end for 20 minutes. After catching their breath, they decided it was time to take a shower. Rachael ran into the bathroom and locked the door laughing, "I get the hot water first and if you're lucky I'll save you some."

Buck didn't mind, with the heat coming on the cold water might feel good after all.

As they pulled out of the parking spot in the red car, Buck and Rachael made their way to the Strip. The cell phone Buck was carrying started to ring; handing the phone to Rachael she opened it and answered the call. After identifying herself Linda said, "Rachael, Metro found the 63 Chevy gold Impala at a place outside of town, near the North Las Vegas airport. So, nobody knows what kind of vehicle the Calderon brothers are driving right now."

"That's good to know," replied Rachael. "Thanks for the update, call us when you have any other information."

"Not a problem, be careful out there" Linda said emphatically.

"Don't worry we will," Rachael said.

Rachael passed on the information to Buck about the car being found. Buck looked concerned now, knowing that the brothers could be anywhere. Buck looked at Rachael, "I have an idea that might work in our favor."

"What is this idea you have, Buck," she asked, wondering what he was talking about.

"Well, how about instead of them hunting us and we not knowing where the brothers are. How about we draw them out and force them into a confrontation with us where we set the ground rules."

Rachael thought about it for a second, "How do we draw them out?"

"It's rather simple, we let them find us and then we drive out of town. And as they follow us we take them out. When the brothers show themselves, we pick them up and turn them over to the FBI and Metro," Buck said, mulling it over in his mind.

The Calderon brothers had pictures of Buck and Rachael and were aware that they would be hard to follow without knowing where they were staying while in town. All they could do was sit and wait at the federal building, hoping they would show up there. The brothers spotted the two of them when they were coming out of the meeting with Linda. They followed close by as Buck drove his car all over the Las Vegas Valley, but were spooked by the Crown Victoria that was following Buck and Rachael also. Not knowing who was in the Crown Victoria, they left and went back to their room all the while trying to figure out their next move.

The Calderon brothers were raised in Bogota, Columbia. They had survived by stealing from people and small jobs for the cartel at first. Working their way up by being good at whatever job was given them. The brothers proved their worth by getting rid of the human problems for the cartel in Columbia. They moved up from being enforcers in Columbia to being enforcers in the United States by helping with the distribution of the drugs from

Columbia. Doing their jobs well by getting rid of the competition and setting up their own drug network to facilitate the new dealers and new drugs coming into the U.S. via Old Mexico. The brothers decided not to sell the drugs and found there was more money in ensuring the drug flow by taking out the competition on the streets or going to different places as henchmen or bodyguards for the important drug suppliers and sometimes drug mules. Working together, they built their reputations as being efficient in getting things done, no matter who got in their way or whatever the challenge. Sanchez liked the brothers because they were home boys from the same town in Columbia. He hired them full time to work for him as enforcers for his west coast operations based in Los Angeles. They would sit around the pool where the girls were dressed in bikinis and swimming in the pool as eye candy for Sanchez's friends and family. Watching the whole time for any threat to their boss and swiftly taking out that perceived threat without thinking twice about it. California agreed with the brother's way of life. Fancy clothes and fast cars were number one on their list of must haves. Yes, life in America was good to them, the money the cars and the women were good to the brothers, and they showed their appreciation by being good at enforcing the rules for Sanchez.

Now that Sanchez was in jail for being an accomplice to Ice Man in Nevada, he needed the brothers to get him out of the jam he was in. Sanchez figured if he got rid of the two that captured him the case against him would disappear. By getting rid of Buck and Rachael, his drug empire would continue to grow and keep making money for him. The brothers would see to that by taking care of the problem for him. For Sanchez, the problem would go away, and life would return back to normal for him in California.

Because of Sanchez being good in the drug business in California, this attracted the FBI and DEA who were now trying to nail him on any charge they could find to stop him. Sanchez was smart because he made sure his hands would never get dirty in his drug empire. Nothing could be traced back to him in any way, except being with Ice Man in Nevada, with dead bodies all around him. This is what the FBI had been looking for, and with the assistance of Buck and Rachael, they finally got him. It would take months to sort this all out for Sanchez, all the while being stuck in jail waiting for the court date.

With Sanchez sitting in jail waiting, the FBI and DEA started putting together their case against him. The agencies knew that if he walked this time they may never get another chance to nail him. Therefore, their job would be to make sure all the I's were dotted, and the T's were crossed. For Sanchez, being in jail was a minor inconvenience. He could still run his empire from here but it would take a little longer to do so. Plus, there was always the competition in his ranks, trying to take over his empire. This was typical in the day of life for Sanchez, but now that he was in jail, it would be harder to enforce his rules. Already, there was talk on the street and along the west coast of him being in jail and not ever coming out. The powers that be in the cartel were even looking at replacing him just in case he didn't get out of jail. Sanchez knew he had to get back out on the street to show he was still in charge, no matter what it took to do it. So far, the two that put him in here had been incredibly lucky and were still alive. The manpower he lost for his attempted hits, was higher than he had expected to pay. Hence, the Calderon brothers were brought in to clean it up for him. It was just a matter of time before it would be completed and he'd be back on the street again running his business as usual.

Buck and Rachael now knew anybody in any car could be the brothers coming after them. It was only a matter of time before the brothers would try to take them out, and it was only a matter of time before they would have to shoot or be shot. Buck's idea of drawing the brothers out was basically a good idea, however that being said, drawing them out into the daylight would be the problem. How to catch the brothers so that they could be found out and eliminated, was the real issue in this game of cat and mouse that Buck and Rachael were now playing.

Buck figured that with the FBI and Metro as their backup, it was a little easier for their safety. But the risk was real for all concerned, suppose the backup didn't get there in time or what would happen if the money Sanchez was paying was more than their consciences could handle. He had to assume that both he and Rachael were on their own in this situation, and acted accordingly. As Buck drove down the I-15 in town, he was constantly checking his rearview mirror and looking at every car as if it were a threat to them.

The Calderon brothers were perplexed by the one car following their targets. Were they back up for the two or were they competition against the brothers? Not knowing who they were, they decided to take the car out of the equation so that they could complete the hit without interference. So, this morning they headed back out on the street looking for their target. The Calderon brothers found the red car that Buck and Rachael were driving and waited for the two to show themselves. Having followed them from the court house to their hotel, the brothers decided to wait until Buck and Rachael were on the road again before attempting to take them out. First things first, the Crown Victoria had to be dealt with.

This morning, Buck and Rachael decided to go to Mt. Charleston and check out the scenic sights of the mountain retreat. Only 30 minutes away from Las Vegas and 20 degrees cooler, as it says in the flyers, the view of the city from Mt. Charleston was beautiful, especially at night. With the lodge, up there on the mountain, it was a quick getaway from the rat race of the city. There was hiking and camping and skiing for the winter enthusiast, and just plain fun, it was a nice break from the city. Buck thought if they could get the brothers to follow them up here, the road to Mt. Charleston, being more isolated, would make it easier to see who was following them. As they stopped to get food stuffs for the trip, Buck stood inside the convenience store and looked out the window. At first, he didn't see anything, looking for the car that the brothers were driving wasn't easy. But as he kept scanning the streets, one of the vehicles he had spotted was parked on the street across from the intersection. He kept watching to see if the car was waiting for the light to turn green to proceed through the intersection. It didn't, Buck now watched it more intently, eventually it continued on through the intersection and disappeared. The brothers had seen Buck looking through the window at them and decided to continue driving to throw him off so they wouldn't be discovered. Buck made a mental note of the SUV and waited for Rachael to finish paying for the groceries.

As Buck left with Rachael he said, "I think we may have some visitors following us."

"Where are they," Rachael asked, alarmed by what Buck said.

"I'm not for sure, but there was a white SUV parked on the other side of the intersection watching us, at least it looked that way to me," Buck said, with some uncertainty.

Rachael continued walking with the groceries' in her hands and not looking around, "We'll know for sure in a little while, won't we?"

Once back in the car, Buck and Rachael checked their semi-autos to make sure they were loaded and ready. They pulled out of the convenience store parking lot and headed onto I -15 again to take the turn off for Mt. Charleston. As they made the turn off and started up the road heading west towards the mountains, Buck and Rachael kept scanning the road in front of them and behind them.

The brothers were already on their way back from passing through the intersection when they saw the red car get on the freeway in the opposite direction that they were traveling. Making a U turn in the middle of the road, they started catching up to Buck and Rachael. The brother that wasn't driving was looking for the Crown Victoria as they made their way up the road. The Crown Victoria was about a quarter mile behind Buck and Rachael when the white SUV passed them on the road. The brother on the passenger side of the SUV rolled down his window and shot into the hood of the car, forcing the FBI agents to slow down and maneuver out of the way of the SUV. The shotgun the brothers had used on the car had little effect on the reinforced motor of the Crown Vitoria. The FBI agents called in asking for backup in their pursuit of the white SUV. The

Metro detectives, who were following Buck and Rachael as well, heard the call on the police radio in their car and responded to the call saying that they were behind the FBI vehicle in pursuit, as well. The SUV was now being chased by the FBI and Metro units as it made its way to Rachael and Buck. The brothers were looking for the red car. One of the FBI agents called Linda to let her know of the pursuit. She in turn called Rachael and let her know what was going on and that two cars were in the chase after the white SUV.

Rachael let Buck know that his hunch was right and that the white SUV was on its way to try and catch them. Buck thought for a moment and stopped the car in the middle of the road blocking both lanes. Buck and Rachael got out of the car and facing down the road with their weapons pulled from the other side of the car, waited for the white SUV to come.

The brothers were watching the cars that were following them and wondering who they belonged to. But the SUV had a head start on them and would get to the red car before the two cars following, could get to them. Buck was directing traffic around where their car was sitting in the middle of the road. Off in the distance Buck saw the white SUV coming fast towards them. The brothers could tell from the distance that the red car was blocking both lanes of travel. As they got closer to where Buck and Rachael were waiting for them, they realized they were in a pickle with nowhere to go except into the desert. Slowing down would bring the other two cars up faster and speeding up they would hit the red car. With no other alternative, the brothers chose to go into the desert turning off the highway. They hit the desert doing about 60 miles an hour, as they left the road and went into the desert. The SUV hit a sagebrush mound, and being high centered, wasn't able to stay upright, causing the SUV to roll three times before landing on its wheels. The brothers were not buckled in and both of them went flying through the windshield and landed in the desert on some rocks. Both of the brothers were cut up pretty bad but were alive, at least for the moment. By now, the FBI and Metro units arrived on the scene. Getting out of their cars, they ran into the desert with Buck and Rachael, to survey the damage from the wreck.

Buck found both brothers lying on the ground outside their vehicle, he quickly checked them to make sure that they had no weapons. Rachael, with her gun out, stood guard as he did this. The two FBI agents, and Frank and his partner, looked at both of the brothers lying on the ground. One of the brother's legs was bent in the wrong direction with the femur bone sticking out, as he lay there. The other brother, who was able to move, had a gash on his head and part of his scalp was lying on the ground next to him. He was completely out of it, not knowing where he was at the time.

Buck looked at them. "You know if these guys were animals we would shoot them to put them out of their misery."

Frank chuckled, "They are animals as far as I'm concerned."

The two FBI agents nodded their heads in agreement. "Amen to that brother."

The ambulance arrived taking both of the brothers to the hospital. However, before they left the scene, one of the FBI agents had the forensics team take pictures of the brothers for verification and as part of the case against Sanchez. Once the area had been cleaned up, and the white SUV was towed to the impound lot, Buck and Rachael were able to go to Mt. Charleston and have dinner with the FBI agents and Metro detectives. The report would have to wait until tomorrow morning, right now it was a time to celebrate the capture of the brothers. The charges against them would be a mile long, and would entail the murder of Mark Lopez, the driver, and grand theft auto on the 63 Chevy Impala, just to start the ball rolling.

Rachael called Linda, "The brothers are out of business for the rest of their lives. And we're okay, no one got hurt except the bad guys."

Linda sounded relieved by the phone call from Rachael, "I'll see you two tomorrow."

Tonight, the food bill was on Buck and Rachael. And of course, the detectives and special agents ordered their favorite steak dinners, with everybody's favorite dessert, death by chocolate with a scoop of ice cream on the side. At the end of the dinner Buck and Rachael thanked them again for backing them up all the way through this ordeal. They all shook hands with Buck, and got a hug from Rachael and left for the night to go home.

Buck looked up into the night sky and smiled, "Look at the stars up there aren't they beautiful tonight?"

"Yes, they are beautiful tonight," replied Rachael, snuggling closer to Buck.

Buck looked at her, "I love you and I'm sure glad you're here with me."

"Me too," Rachael said, kissing him. "You know what, it's cold out here."

"Yeah, ain't it great," said Buck.

As they made their way down the mountain back into Vegas they stopped at Gared and Tina's house and told them the good news about the brothers and Sanchez along with Ice Man. Everybody sat spellbound as Buck and Rachael detailed their adventures to the group. Evans and Linda were sitting there listening to it all and finally said, "I guess this wraps up the cases against all of the bad guys now, huh?"

"Not quite yet, we still need to visit Sanchez and talk to him while were still here," Buck said rather cryptically.

Rachael looked at Linda and Evans with a questioning look on her face and shrugged her shoulders. When all of the stories were done and everybody was headed to bed, Buck and Rachael left the house and headed back to their hotel room. Getting ready for bed, Buck looked at Rachael, "I think we can go home now."

"That sounds so good right now, sleeping in our own bed, in our own home. I wonder what that would be like?" Rachael lamented

"I don't remember exactly how to get home from here do you? It's been so long," questioned Buck.

"I don't remember either, but I'm willing to try and find our way back home" Rachael said, falling asleep. Buck crawled in next her and was out just as fast. Tonight would be the first night that they would sleep soundly, knowing that no one was after them.

Chapter XIV

The next day Buck and Rachael were in Linda's office waiting for her, and as she walked in the door Buck and Rachael stood up to greet her.

After the hugs and pleasantries were done, Buck asked Linda, "Can I borrow some of the pictures from the wreck out in the desert? I'll only need them for a little while and I'll bring them back to you."

"Yes, you may, in fact, keep them if you wish," said Linda. "We have plenty of others. By the way, why do you want them?"

"Well it's like this; I want to show the pictures to Sanchez and Ice Man, and give a special message with it," smirked Buck.

"I wish I could be the fly on the wall, after this visit, with you guys" laughed Linda.

"Not to worry I'll fill you in," Rachael said, chuckling.

Buck and Rachael left the office and headed to Metro to visit Sanchez. Waiting in one of the rooms for Sanchez, Buck and Rachael sat in the chairs across the table. When Sanchez showed up, he smiled at Buck and Rachael, "To what do I owe the pleasure of your visit?"

"Oh, nothing all that important, but we wanted to talk to you about the Calderon brothers you hired to kill us," said Buck.

"Oh, by the way, here are the pictures of the brothers after the accident. They're doing better now though," Rachael said, smiling.

After looking at the pictures, he threw them back at Buck. "I don't know what you're talking about. What did you say their names were?" Sanchez asked, playing dumb.

"You know, the Calderon brothers," said Rachael.

"You remember, you sent for them from L.A. I can't believe you don't remember them. That's alright, because they remember you very well. In fact, they told the FBI that you hired them to kill us. Now it's your word against the two of theirs. Gee, I wonder who the jury is going to believe, you or those two," Buck said, sarcastically.

Sanchez's face started to turn red at the news, and his fists tightened as he sat there glaring at Buck and Rachael.

"Now, Now, Now, you need to be careful about your blood pressure, you might have a heart attack," Rachael said, mocking Sanchez.

"I'm not worried, they can be gone just like

anybody else," Sanchez said, smiling.

"The only problem you might have, is that you got to find them first," Buck said, in a matter of fact tone.

"And by the way, we're staying for your arraignment tomorrow," said Rachael. "So, you get to see us again, real soon. Bad luck with the Calderon brothers testifying against you, isn't it?"

Sanchez was quiet as Buck and Rachael got up and left the room. "See you tomorrow, Sanchez," said Rachael.

Sanchez was walked back to his cell and asked the guard if he could make a phone call.

Later that evening, Sanchez reached out to his partners in Los Angeles. The problem was, nobody would accept his calls anymore. For Sanchez, being in charge of the west coast drug operations was over. The next day Sanchez got a hold of the FBI, "What do I got to do in order to get my jail sentence reduced?"

Linda sat in the meeting with the Federal attorneys as they offered Sanchez a deal if he would turn states evidence against his previous employers. Sanchez knew he would be killed in prison and would never see freedom again. Sanchez agreed to turn states evidence against Ice Man and against the cartel. The arraignment for Sanchez was cancelled because of the new deal with the FBI.

Buck and Rachael, upon hearing the news, were put out a little bit. However, seeing the bigger picture and understanding how the game was played, they knew it was for the best.

Once Ice Man knew he had been turned on, he wanted the same deal as Sanchez got. He in turn told the FBI about the drug operations in Las Vegas and about the setup of Mako and anything that would make him more valuable to the FBI.

Buck and Rachael made another visit to Gared and Tina's place, one more time to touch base with Miguel and the rest of the kids, and of course to see Evans. During their visit, they talked about heading back to Arizona and getting back to their own lives again. You know, the boring stuff of being a sheriff in a county nobody knew of or cared about.

The kids were able to get their UNLV professors to allow them to take the classes they missed as incompletes and be allowed to take them through the summer, that is with the help of the FBI coming down to explain their part in catching Ice Man and the others.

Tim and Jennifer promised to never go after any airplanes flying low in the desert anymore on threat of Buck and Rachael coming back to hurt them.

Miguel, with Marissa, realizing that they were heading back to Arizona shortly, told his mom and dad goodbye and that he would see them when school was on break.

Buck and Rachael, looking at the two of the kids standing, there said, "You make a good-looking couple."

Miguel and Marissa blushed at this.

"Marissa, your welcome at our home anytime down in Arizona," Rachael said, smiling.

"Thank you," Marissa smiled, at being accepted by Miguel's parents.

That night Linda, and Evans, who was able to move around by now, took them to dinner in the Mandalay Bay Hotel and there they said their goodbyes.

By now, Buck and Rachael were ready to go home to Arizona, and with everybody turning on everybody, the FBI and Metro police department would be busy for quite a while with all of the arrests being made from the information given to them by Ice Man and Sanchez. Buck and Rachael went to Bill's towing and car maintenance shop to drop off the loaner car back to Bill. When they got there, Bill told one of his mechanics to go get the truck from the yard. When the mechanic brought it out to them, Buck and Rachael didn't recognize the truck as their own. Bill had the bullet holes fixed and the engine replaced and the truck cleaned up. All Buck could do was stand there and look at the truck. For the first time in Buck's life he was speechless. Rachael did all of the talking for him while Buck went and looked at the truck, touching the side of it and opening the doors to look inside.

Rachael smiled, watching Buck, "Bill you have made Buck a very happy, happy man. Thank you for what you have done."

Bill handed the keys to Buck, "It's all yours and thanks for what you done for our town."

Buck shook his hand and got in and started the truck engine, and as he listened to it he smiled and sat there holding the steering wheel with both hands. Rachael got into the truck and after saying their goodbyes to Bill and the mechanics.

Buck didn't say a word until he was across the bridge that spanned the Colorado River just below Hoover Dam as they hit the Arizona state line. Looking at Rachael all he said was, "Were going home, this time for sure."

Epilogue

Buck and Rachael did finally get home safely and the sheriff's office was boring and unknown to a lot of people that passed through the county onto other places. They had two kids, a boy, and a girl, named Chad and Eleanor. Both of the kids were the apple of their parent's eyes. Linda and Evans were the godparent to both of the kids. Buck and Rachael were offered positions as FBI agents which they turned down, saying that they preferred the slow life in Arizona. In turn, the FBI awarded Buck and Rachael their highest medals of Valor, which they hung on the wall in their offices to show off.

Miguel and Marissa came and visited Buck and Rachael's house every break from school that they could. They eventually married after graduating from UNLV and moved to Phoenix. Miguel ended up working for the Phoenix Police department as a police officer on the streets and after two years made detective, working in their narcotics unit. Marissa had three children, one boy and two girls, named Peter. Sarah, and

Jennifer, to which Buck and Rachael are the youngest and proudest grandparents in all of Arizona.

Evans and Linda never went back to Washington, they stayed there in Las Vegas and worked the cases that Sanchez and Ice Man opened up for them. The FBI office was expanded to accommodate all of the cases they had going there. Evans recovered from his wound and directed the work at the new FBI office. The work accomplished by Linda and Evans, during this time, got them the highest medals from the FBI, DEA, and the local police departments. Linda and Evans ended up having a child of their own, a boy who they named after Evans, with Buck and Rachael in return being the godparents.

Sanchez was a gold mine of information for the FBI and local police in Los Angeles and San Francisco and other cities in California. The information that Sanchez gave them shut down the entire organization of the west coast distribution of drugs and it took another year for the cartel to recover from the testimony of Sanchez.

By then, the in house fighting of the dealers and gangs involved, took their toll on the drug dealing and was never quite the same after that.

For a short time, the west coast was drug free, simply because the deliveries were intercepted by the local police departments all along the corridors.

Ice Man, turning on the locals in Las Vegas, assisted in the apprehension of the dealers and distributors in the all of Nevada and parts of Utah and Arizona.

Both Ice Man and Sanchez were put into the witness protection program and moved to North Dakota to live out their days as gentlemen farmers after they served their reduced sentences in Club Fed, in the Fort Walton Beach facility.

In total, 36 arrests of key members in California in the west coast network netted another 200 arrests in dealers and other low life characters working the streets throughout California, Washington, Oregon, and Nevada. The actual total count went well over what the papers showed, simply because of the other ongoing investigations that were still classified.

Mako, having nothing to offer, went straight to prison to serve his 20 years outside of Las Vegas, and at last report, was somebody's love partner inside the prison.

Frankie Diamond, whose real name was George Abbot, was picked up from his penthouse where he was recuperating from the gunshots to his knees, and placed under arrest based upon the testimony of Ice Man. He was sent to Club Fed to serve his life sentence for the contract hits he made for Ice man along with the Racketeer Influenced and Corrupt Organizations Act (RICO) charges stemming from the kickbacks from Ice Man. Frankie Diamond would be confined to a wheel chair for the rest of his life. He would, eventually, be moved to a state prison.

The Calderon brothers were sent to the federal maximum-security prison in Florence, Colorado to serve their life sentences. They were charged with attempted murder of federal agents, admitting to the attempted hit on Buck and Rachael, and the murder of Mark Lopez. Because of the accident, the one brother walked with a limp for the rest of his life and the other brother ended up having traumatic brain injury and could not function on his own. His bother would take care of him until he died, while in prison.

Gared and Tina, were given letters of appreciation from the FBI and Metro police department for their part in helping the kids and assisting Evans recover from his wound. Every once in a while, Linda and Evans will swing by with their son and have dinner at their place. Hannah was given a letter of appreciation for specifically helping Evans while he recuperated. She went on to become an FBI agent after graduating from college, and Quantico (FBI academy), eventually, coming to work in the Las Vegas office to work for Evans and Linda.

And last but not least, Sherron was given a letter of appreciation for her work and surviving the attempt on her life while doing her duties. Sherron would later marry a young man who would take her away to live in Utah where they would spend their time refurbishing old houses for fun and profit and live happily ever after with her friends and family around her.